D1489741

THUNDER AND ACID

A POST-APOCALYPTIC SURVIVAL THRILLER

HARLEY TATE

THUNDER AND ACID

Falling temperatures and acid rain. A sanctuary that's not all it seems. A family caught in the middle.

Welcome to *Falling Skies*. Do you have what it takes to survive?

After an asteroid crashes into the Atlantic Ocean, Caleb Machert risks everything to transport his family to safety. But two weeks later, he's having doubts. Are the soldiers he's working alongside rebuilding the United States, or tearing it apart?

Elizabeth spends her days prepping food, cleaning toilets, and failing to make friends. While hauling recycling, she overhears a soldier blaming her husband for a failed mission. If the general believes it, then Caleb's in grave danger.

Reeling from an unexpected loss, Lana is determined to never let anyone down again. She's intent on becoming not just a soldier, but a fighting machine. When faced with a do or die situation, her training is put to the test. This time, she might pay the ultimate price.

It's a race against the clock for the Macherts before freezing temperatures and acid rain are the least of their problems.

Thunder and Acid is book two in *Falling Skies*, a post-apocalyptic thriller series following ordinary people struggling to survive when a meteor strike plunges the United States into chaos.

Subscribe to Harley's newsletter to receive updates about new releases, free content, and more.

www.harleytate.com/subscribe

PROLOGUE

Cheyenne Mountain Complex
  Colorado Springs, CO
  Monday, June 14th 10:05 am MST

Thomas Daniels ran his campaign for President of the United States as a man of God. Raised Methodist, he attended church regularly for most of his life. But if he was honest with himself, he'd only ever been marginally religious. It was family tradition, that was all.

He believed in the distant sort of way that plenty of people did, but wouldn't have called himself *devout*. Not the way his constituents were led to believe.

There were times on the campaign trail when he had misgivings about his proclamations of faith, crafted by some speech writer with polling data in mind. Would God bring him low for his exaggerations? Would he be outed as a fraud? But it never happened, he was elected, and was a *good* president.

According to the polls, anyway.

Daniels stared into the middle distance, somewhere between the end of the desk and the concrete wall of his presidential office in Cheyenne Mountain. Maybe Hell wasn't a metaphor. Maybe all those speeches where he proclaimed his belief in an active God weren't exaggerations at all. Maybe God really did take a personal hand in mortal affairs and humanity had been found wanting in His judgment.

Hell, a pastor explained to him once, was not an eternal existence of pain and agony, not a lake of fire, or a pit of endless torture. Instead, it was simply the absence of God. A place where God's light couldn't reach. A place of unending hopelessness.

"...nearly fifteen degrees in the last two weeks, and temperatures are still falling nationwide." The voice of President Daniels's chief of staff filtered into his consciousness. "Mister President?"

Daniels blinked away his distraction and turned to the younger man. "I'm listening, Pete."

Pete Camby closed the folder in his hands and laid it on the desk between them. Daniels reached across the plain aluminum. With no more gravitas than a child's desk in an elementary classroom, his current desk was a poor substitute for the desk in the Oval Office.

Made from oak timbers of the British ship H.M.S. Resolute as a gift to President Hayes from Queen Victoria in 1880, the Resolute Desk as it came to be known, held a special place in Daniels's heart. He used to run his hands over the carved wood and imagine countless past presidents doing the same. It gave him strength. Grounding. Gravitas.

He palmed the cold metal and shrank inside.

"Would you like me to have some coffee brought, sir? If you'll forgive me, you seem…"

Weak? He exhaled when Pete didn't continue. "Coffee would be fine, thank you."

Pete muttered the order into his radio before leveling a long, concerned look on him.

Daniels leaned back in his chair. "Say what's on your mind. I need your candidness."

Pete hesitated a moment, but Daniels picked him as campaign manager for the same reasons he made an excellent chief of staff. He considered his words before he spoke, and what he said was always worth hearing.

"One of the most important jobs you have at the moment, sir," Pete explained carefully, "is to not get mired in despair. There's not a whole lot keeping our people together right now—the people here, in this facility, I mean—except their faith in your leadership."

"Oh, is *that* my most important job?" Daniels rubbed the bridge of his nose where the longest headache of his life had taken up permanent residence. "Here I thought it was to carve out policy for a new kind of world none of us ever expected to live in. Silly me."

Pete's jaw flexed, but he recognized his friend's dry humor even if it was darker than usual. "*One of*," he repeated. "I'm only mentioning it because people are beginning to notice."

Daniels turned away from his old friend. Of course, they were noticing. How could they not? Every day was a new report, worse than the last. The only bit of good news had been when the ash stopped falling and rain cleared the air enough that Americans could finally take a full breath outside without suffocating.

But the rain kept falling. And the sky began to shake with thunderous fury. The National Oceanic and Atmospheric Administration projected storms on the horizon unlike anything seen in human history: lightning storms lasting days, windstorms scraping entire towns off the map, off-the-chart tornados. Already, hurricanes relentlessly pummeled the east coast with no sign of slowing.

And the cold... the cold was coming.

"Then my anger shall be kindled against them in that day," Daniels began, his voice soft and strained, "and I will forsake them, and I will hide my face from them, and they shall be devoured, and many evils and troubles shall befall them; so that they will say in that day, are not these evils come upon us, because our God is not among us?"

The lines around Pete's mouth deepened as his brow furrowed. "Psalms?"

"Deuteronomy." He shook his head, mystified at his ability to recall the verse after all this time. "Funny what sticks in your head when you're not paying attention. I think I first heard that when I was sixteen."

"With all due respect," Pete offered as he raised his eyes again, "God didn't do this. It was just a random act of nature. One that's happened before, several times, and one that will almost certainly happen again. This isn't some kind of punishment. It's a disaster, and one that we'll get through. One that we *must* get through. But it will be a lot harder if you lose hope."

"I haven't lost hope." Daniels meant every word. "I'm just a little maudlin, Pete. You've got to indulge me that. At least in private."

"Yes, sir," Pete agreed, as the door to the office opened, and Lieutenant Marcus Yaeger entered with a mug. Pete waved him over. "Come on in, Lieutenant."

For the few seconds that it took to deliver the drink, Daniels ensured that he didn't look hopeless or tired. He squared his shoulders, straightened his back, and plastered the calm, competent expression he'd mastered way back on the debate stage in college all over his face.

He accepted the mug from the young Lieutenant with a grateful nod. "I do appreciate it, Marcus." The part of his mind that had spent thirty years playing politics shuffled automatically through a mental dossier on the man and plucked out the necessary information. "How's Rosalind doing lately? I don't think I've asked in a few days. She was having some respiratory problems before, was she not?"

Lieutenant Yaeger's eyes lit up somewhat, and he smiled slightly at the mention of his wife. "She's doing better, sir. It was just a cold, the doc said. Nothing serious."

"You let her know I'm glad to hear that." Daniels sipped the coffee before he nodded approval and smiled up at the Lieutenant. "This is just perfect. Exactly what I needed."

Pete dismissed the man and turned to Daniels with a half-smile as he retrieved the folder from the desk and opened it again.

"What's that grin for?"

"I'm just reminded why I agreed to manage your campaign for congress all those years ago. And why I'm glad to serve with you now, Tom." After a moment, his smile fell, and his eyes grew serious.

Back to business. Daniels waved him on. "Go ahead."

Instead of reading from the folder, Pete lowered his voice slightly, and glanced at the closed door to the office. "The people who have noticed your... *maudlin* mood, are the same ones saying that you're too nervous to act decisively. They want more action from you. A show of strength. Madame Speaker has been particularly insistent."

"They want me to declare martial law," the president clarified. Two weeks before, the mere thought boiled his blood. Now it just made him tired.

Pete glanced down at the folder, flipped the page, and licked his lips. "We've lost contact with a number of rescue operations, communications outposts, and checkpoints. Most of them are in the Appalachian Mountain region, right around where North Carolina, Virginia, and Tennessee meet."

"Weather related? It's one of the hardest hit areas due to the impact. Weren't there wildfires at the beginning?"

Pete nodded. "Yes, and there are still some fires as far

as our latest intelligence shows. But we were in contact with several a few days ago, using the radio-satellite relay system we patched together. To our knowledge, that system is still functioning."

"Who do we still have contact with out there?"

"I can find out from General Ainsworth."

"Do that," Daniels agreed. "And see who he can send out to investigate. Intelligence gathering *only*. Make that clear; I just want to know what's going on out there."

Pete scribbled a note. "He's going to ask about authorization of force. In the event of... *trouble*."

He'd been going to say *in the event of insurgents*, Daniels knew. That word had been gaining traction over the past couple of weeks. All around the country, amid the deepening cold, and the storms, and the fires, a dozen little fiefdoms had tried to take root.

A portion of Chicago, St. Louis, even one in Colorado were all attempting to create order out of chaos. At this point, even President Daniels had to admit that the people leading these various communities sounded more and more like would-be warlords.

Martial law would only make it worse. He understood the impulse, the need to clamp down and force order to happen. It was the same impulse a parent had when confronted with an unruly child. But that kind of paternalism did more harm than good. He believed that. He'd seen it happen before in other nations and knew of dozens of other times it had failed throughout history.

Daniels leaned forward and curled a fist above the cold metal desktop. "Make it clear to the general that no force is authorized until we have a better understanding of what is happening. Even if it's another militia—observe and report *only*. Give Ainsworth an inch and he'll take ten miles but only admit to three of them. I'm not about to let him off the leash."

Pete's lips thinned, and he made another note before turning the page. "Speaking of militias, we've made inroads with the group outside Jackson, Wyoming. They're asking for…"

Daniels listened patiently to the rest of the report, managing to keep his attention focused for the most part.

But the more he heard, the more a weight settled on his shoulders, heavier, somehow, than when he was sworn into office. And he couldn't help himself from thinking of another verse. One that came unbidden to his thoughts. Part of a Psalm that his grandmother from the Pentecostal side of the family had taught him.

Answer me quickly, O Lord, my spirit fails, do not hide Your face from me, or I will become like those who go down to the pit.

He only hoped they weren't there yet, and there was still time to return to grace.

CHAPTER ONE

Piney Creek Road, Lansing, NC
   Monday, June 14th 3:57pm EST

The last can of baked beans weighed heavy in
Lerlaine Cobb's hands. Tears skidded down her dry
cheeks as she stared at the empty cabinets. Her shoulders
shook. Pain spread across her chest as she muffled her
sobs, hiding from her two boys in the kitchen.

Maddox wailed from the living room, globs of snot
bubbling across his upper lip before dribbling down his
chin. At three years old, he was too young to understand
the ache deep in his belly. Hunger pains. At the first
high-pitched wail, she'd retreated into the kitchen—run
from him, if she was being honest—because there was
precious little holding her together these days. He didn't
need to see her falling apart.

Lerlaine stole a glance at the bouncy seat resting on
the floor. Hunter *wasn't* crying, and in a way, that was

worse. Ten months old were *supposed* to cry when they were hungry. But after her milk dried up and the store ran out of formula...

He was weak and getting weaker.

One can of beans. Half a canister of dry formula. The water ran for a while, pumped from the shared well out back. But then the ground shook in a quake strong enough to collapse the whole dang house and the tap hadn't run after that. She eyed the half a jug of water on the counter through her tears.

Enough of that. Get it together.

She wiped her eyes and ran a tongue across her dry lips as she snatched the can opener off the counter. Her hands moved automatically, almost numb, and the sound of shearing metal hurt her ears. Everything was painful now.

When the sky lit with streaks of fire, then the ash rained down, and the wind picked up and flattened half the town, she'd thought God favored her little family somehow. That the blood of Jesus Christ had washed over them in their sleep and spared them. It seemed like a miracle.

Almost nothing in Lansing survived, but there she was—her windows boarded up and her roof patched with some old plywood from the shed, but otherwise intact. She'd made it. Her children had *made* it.

Hurricanes pummeled the coast her entire life. They'd be on the news a few times a year—this or that city flooded, houses destroyed, whole towns sometimes. Inland towns full of displaced people, strangers whose whole lives were destroyed in an instant; in one terrible, hellish moment, everything was gone.

But then someone showed up. FEMA, the Red Cross, the national guard. Neighbors and volunteers. People flooded in as the flood water receded, cleared the wreckage, and made way for rebuilding to begin. For weeks and weeks, sometimes months, it was all that was on the news—*Small-town America, still a mess, but getting better. Story at ten.*

After the miracle, after the rocks and the fire and the wind and the awful ash that had covered everything and choked the air... After the electricity failed, and the water stopped flowing, she'd told herself that if she just waited, they would come.

All those helpers and heroes always on the news— they would come, and she would be saved. Someone would help her rebuild. She would help *others* rebuild. They would tell their story on the nightly news of survival and optimism. Of hope against all odds. Of salvation.

She poured half the can of beans into two bowls. Most for Maddox, a few spoonfuls for herself. She'd gladly give him everything if it meant he'd survive, but if she starved...Well, it wouldn't serve him any, would it?

Once in a while, when the boys were sleeping, she imagined that she was in front of a TV camera, wrapped in a scratchy wool blanket with Maddox clinging to her leg and Hunter cradled in one arm. "It's just awful," she'd say, "everything that's happened. We've all lost so much. But I just give thanks to God that I have my family. The rest of it... it hurts to lose it. Everything's gone, you know? But we were blessed. We survived, and we are *blessed*."

The cameraman would pan out, a wide shot of the debris field in front of her house, and the reporter would sign off with hope tilting her voice higher at the end.

Each time she had that fantasy, Lerlaine hated herself for it. But it gave her comfort. More than praying did. So, she went back to it again and again, hating herself a little more each time for the delusion. No one was coming. There would be no benevolent stranger knocking on the door.

Reality hit her hard and unforgiving. There would be no cameras. No helpers. No scratchy FEMA blanket. Just *him*.

She closed her eyes and swallowed the sob that almost got past her lips. For several seconds she choked on it, until the convulsion passed, and she could wipe her eyes again and turn away from the counter with the two bowls. Maddox still carried on, but he'd quiet down once she put food in front of him.

At least long enough to eat.

In the dim living room, she found her little pumpkin red-faced on the couch, his face wet and snotty as he gasped for air. He'd been good for her and stayed where she'd put him but hadn't been happy about it.

Now, he reached up for her, his little fingers grasping at air. *Save me*, he said. *I don't know what's wrong, but please, Mama, save me from it*. Not with words. Never with words. The doctors warned her, what seemed like a lifetime ago, that he would need time. Time to speak, time to learn. Time they no longer possessed.

"I'm here, Pumpkin." She tried to soothe him with her voice, attempting to hide the raw scrape of her parched throat. "Mama brought you something to eat. Come on."

She eased the bowls onto the coffee table and slipped her hands under his little shoulders before lifting him onto her lap. Cradling him against her with one arm, she kissed his forehead. He wailed again, the sound stabbing at her ears, and pushed against her as if to get away.

He didn't like being held, and never had. But she kept him on her lap anyway and endured his little fist as he pounded at her shoulder. She sank down by the coffee table and reached for the bowl, tipping it to show him the beans. "See?" she whispered in his ear. "Hungry?"

It was lucky, in a way, that she'd had so many cans. Maddox was picky about what he would eat, like most kids on the spectrum were. Somehow, he'd gotten a taste for baked beans, and she'd just been happy that wars at dinner time lessened, so she'd stocked up.

Maddox's crying eased into a weak kind of mewling, subsiding only when she gave him a spoonful of the beans. He ate in relative silence for a while. She should have relished it—the quiet. But it gave her time to think. About the lack of food. The lack of water. The looming threat of starvation.

She'd held out for as long as she could, but now they had to move or die. There was only one place to go.

His face loomed in her thoughts. Worn ugly from the

sneers and scowls. His voice, always cruel. His fists and how they always seemed to find the best place to land a punch. The way he spit into a can while his eyes crawled over her body.

The awful smell of him when he'd been drinking and pushed himself on her. She shuddered and scraped at the bowl to slip another spoonful of beans into Maddox's mouth.

She hadn't gone far enough away. If she had, she wouldn't have to make this decision now. But she hadn't, and she did. Maddox accepted the last little bit of beans from the bowl.

Hunter twitched in the bouncy seat where he'd been sleeping for much too long. If they didn't go, her children would die ,and she would die with them. Maybe that would be better. The sweet relief of fading away from this life. Maybe they'd be together in heaven. Maybe God had spared them, but only long enough for her to make peace with it.

But the plain fact was that she *hadn't* made peace with it. She wanted to live; wanted her *children* to live. To have a chance to endure long enough to reach the other side. She grabbed her bowl and fed Maddox her share as well before retreating to the kitchen and dumping the remains of the can into the bowl. He ate, gaunt little cheeks ballooning with each bite, until he downed the entire can.

As he finished, she gathered up her courage—or her desperation, maybe, but it didn't matter—and knelt before him with a smile that didn't reach her eyes. "How about we go outside?"

Maddox's hands flapped, and he reached up for her in the same way he had before, his hands opening and closing. *Yes, please, let's go outside!*

Lerlaine dressed him for the cold, wrapped herself in her winter jacket, and layered on a scarf. After easing Hunter into his car carrier, she layered extra blankets on top, shoving down the pain as he opened his tiny dark eyes before suckling at nothing and drifting back to sleep.

She hauled the carrier to the stroller and snugged it down, shoving her emotions down with it. Better to feel nothing than the alternative.

One deep breath at the door, and she threw it open. On any given June afternoon before, the sun would have hit them full in the face, scrunching her eyes and drawing a wail from Maddox. The blast of damp, thick air would frizz her hair and bead sweat across her forehead. Not today.

Instead, it was barely above fifty and dark enough to mimic a cloudy sunset. A distant, dull glow brightened a smudge of sky to the west, but no warmth of sun's rays penetrated the gloom.

Lerlaine began to walk, one hand on the stroller, the other gripping Maddox's tiny hand. He kicked at the ash where it piled on the ground, sending up puffs of what was still loose. A few times, she leaned down to tug his scarf over his face, but he didn't like it and always pulled it down when she looked away.

The world hung still and expectant like a graveyard—

silent, but looming with growing fear. The trees that had made Lansing green for so many summers were now bare, broken, or fallen entirely. As if all the life had drained away.

A memory of Lerlaine's grandmother in the days before she died sprang to mind. She'd always been deathly thin, but she became a skeletal husk in the final days, dry and wan, with brittle hair and cracked skin patchy with sores. Alzheimer's was a cruel mistress.

At twelve, Lerlaine thought it was like her grand-mother had already left, and that her body just hadn't realized it yet. Lansing was like that now. Whatever had made it a *place* was gone, and the rest was just rotting away for lack of anything to keep it alive.

Cars dotted the side of the road, wrecked or clogged by the ash until they choked and sputtered to death. Houses of neighbors she'd known for years were now scattered piles of debris like the towers of blocks Maddox loved to build and kick over. A few bits and pieces standing defiant in the face of the toddler's wrath. Broken, sad reminders of what they'd been.

Thanks to the wind, ash heaped up against anything still standing and caked into every crack and nook. As they walked, chunks of compressed ash dropped almost soundlessly from broken trees, shaken loose by the barest of disturbances to *thwump* to the ground in a puff. The breeze gathered up the new clumps, sending them spin-ning into some new resting place. The little swirls were everywhere, rising and falling like ghosts unsure where they belonged.

When Maddox slowed, his scrawny frame exhausted from walking, Lerlaine picked him up and settled him on her hip. He laid his head against her shoulder, and she hoped that he would sleep, and that her occasional coughing didn't jostle him too much. There wasn't much further to go.

The road turned to dirt the last half mile or so, leading up a scraggly hill. At the end, she stood, heaving for breath, before a double-wide trailer, listening to the hacking growl of a gas generator. A tarp shielded Ray's old race car out front, ash piled in the dips and valleys. She entertained the idea of stealing it for a long time as she calmed her nerves and slowed her breath.

Can't seem too desperate. Not that he wouldn't know. After all, she'd never have come here if she wasn't desperate, right? But she needed at least a scrap of dignity.

Even if she managed to find the keys, which were somewhere inside, no doubt, where would she go? Any direction would be a gamble, and probably one with losing odds. With no food or water, she'd only be delaying the end.

Ray, on the other hand, had a shed full of supplies, a freezer full of meat, and a cupboard packed with jerky and lard. It would be hard, sure. But they would survive here. It would be worth it in the end. Whatever he wanted, it was a price she could pay if it meant her children lived.

She pushed away the fantasy of stealing his car and

knocked on the door. It took almost a minute before the door groaned open. There he was.

Greasy, unkempt hair hung over Ray's bare shoulders. He hadn't shaved in weeks, it looked like. His bloodshot eyes focused on her, full of contempt and hardness. For a long moment he looked her over before he spat a glob of sticky brown sludge into the empty soda bottle in his hand.

The wad of chewing tobacco shifted beneath his lip as he nodded at her. "About damn time. Knew you'd come crawling up here, eventually. Hey kiddo."

Maddox watched Ray uneasily, his fingers tangling in his mother's scarf as Ray showed stained teeth in a smile that Lerlaine only saw as vicious.

"Well, get in," he growled after another few seconds. "You're letting the damned heat out. No wonder you came back. You're too stupid to make it on your own."

Revulsion and pain stirred in Lerlaine's belly, but she forced it down into the pit of her stomach and slipped inside.

It was the only way.

CHAPTER TWO
LANA

Horse Creek Base, New United States
Thursday, June 17th, 7:15 am EST

"Throw your arm over mine when I come in low."
Derek squared off to face Lana, rubber knife in one hand.
"Start with that, okay?"

She nodded and unfocused her eyes the way he'd
instructed when they first started training together in the
mornings, taking all of him in. Her breathing came deep
and easy, and she waited for him to move. But in the span
of a few heartbeats between waiting and the sudden
twitch of his body, she managed to see it all again.

*Jessup, on the ground, blood spattered on the inside of
his mask. That terrible, wet, hacking as his lungs filled
with blood. His eyes, focused on her one moment, then on
nothing the next.* It was so real, so present in her mind,
every detail carved perfectly in front of her, that she
moved on autopilot. Not really seeing Derek at all.

He came in low, like he'd said, one arm at his chest, the other coming upward with the knife toward her gut. Lana stepped into him, twisting to throw her arm over his so that she trapped it against her side. The maneuver left her facing nearly away from him, her hip pressed against his thigh. It was slow and clumsy, but she was learning.

"That's good." He put a hand to her opposite hip and tugged her up a bit. "But you want your hip up here, level with mine. Feel that? How it seems like it fits right there?"

Their hip bones knocked together, and his hand warmed her skin even through the green fatigue pants she wore. His warm breath smelled faintly of toothpaste as he leaned in, the muscle of his arm flexing firm beneath hers. He was solid, dependable. Gentle, but instructive. He liked her. It was obvious.

In the abstract, she admitted he was a good-looking guy, built like a fighter, with that kind of jaw people called 'chiseled' and a dimple on his chin. He kept his hair army regulation buzzed, showing off a nicely shaped head—which wasn't true for all the soldiers in Horse Creek—and his brown eyes were tinged with honey, almost amber. Before, she'd have taken one look at him and declared him *hot*. Combined with his kindness, he was the total package. Lana could see that.

But she didn't feel it. Not one bit. "Okay." She stepped back. "Again. Faster this time."

Derek took a step back and squared up. His body tensed.

Jessup gasped for air.

Lana twisted her body, trapped Derek's arm, her hip thumping against his.

"Perfect. Just like that."

"Again." She let him go. "Faster. Like you mean it."

He rubbed his jaw as he took a step back. "It helps to go slow for a while. So your body can learn to move right. I don't want to hurt you."

"I've been hurt before." She settled into the closest thing to a stance he'd taught her. "I'm not some delicate flower that's gonna get bruised, Derek. Faster."

He pursed his lips, then gave her a nod and bent his knees. This time there was almost no warning. He lurched forward.

Jessup's eyes widened with a last burst of pain before death claimed him. She hadn't told him that she loved him. She didn't know if she did or not, but she hadn't told him, and didn't he want to hear it in the end?

Derek nearly crashed into her. She twisted at the last second, but not before the rubber knife jabbed her chest. She cursed and shoved him away. If it had been a real weapon, he'd have probably punctured a lung. She'd be drowning already, dying before his eyes.

"Again. Fast like that. Like it actually happens."

He didn't take position. Instead, he flipped the knife over, holding it in a reverse grip, and tucked it behind his belt. "Let's take a break."

"I don't need to take a break." Her words came out clipped and mean as she glanced at the clock in the little makeshift training room. "I've got janitorial again in an hour and I'm never going to get off mop duty if I can't fight. Go again."

Derek raised his hands. "Hey—Lana. Calm down. You're shaking. You need a break."

She glanced down at her hands. He wasn't wrong. They practically vibrated. She realized that the rest of her was, as well, and her breathing wasn't coming easy and deep now—it was shallow, sharp. She was practically gasping for air, even though her body didn't feel overworked.

Awful, wet rasping. It filled her ears.

Lana pushed the memory away and dropped to the thin mat on the ground as Derek moved to the wall and picked up a canteen. He took a swig before offering it to her as he sank down beside her. She drank and passed it back to him. "I just need a second."

"No problem." Derek agreed as if it had been her idea all along.

Her eyes combed the room, looking for anything to capture her attention, keep her out of her head. All she saw was the same thing she saw everywhere else, day after day. Concrete walls.

A few new cracks, but nothing apparently dangerous. The quakes came less frequently now, most slight tremors and nothing more. In a way, it was disappointing. Maybe if the quakes had kept up, posing a real threat to the structure, they'd all be outside.

A stab of guilt twisted her insides as she thought about leaving. Jessup *died* to get them here, and gratitude should have filled her heart. But it didn't. She barely felt anything.

Not even attraction to the man who'd been openly flirting with her since she met him and who was probably worth it. It was like all the nerves that responded to those signals were numb. Like her sense of touch, she could see the interaction, remember what it should have felt like on her skin, but the sensation was so dull, it may as well have happened to someone else.

"Any news about topside?" She leaned against the wall.

"If there is," Derek answered, "nobody's tellin' a grunt like me about it. Patrol's pretty tight, we don't range too far. Some comms are up, I think, thanks to your pops, but far as I know nothing's comin' in. You getting a little cabin fever?"

"I just want to know if my future is ever going to be more than canned peaches, concrete walls, and dirty mop water." She kicked at nothing. "We do the same thing every single day. Nothing changes. My dad said the ash stopped falling. Shouldn't we... I don't know, be looking for people, or... whatever happens next?"

He rocked back a bit, nodding. "I guess at some point we will." He shrugged, and glanced around the room himself, like there was an answer written somewhere. "I mean, the general's got a plan, you know? He's gonna build us back up, but it'll take time and it'll be hard. Probably means a lot of canned peaches, but not forever."

He grinned at her like they shared a joke, but Lana failed to muster even a weak smile in response.

Derek's gaze fell. "Anyway... we just gotta stick by it, follow the plan. Trust him. He's gonna whip this country into shape, make everything better than it was before."

Lana forced herself not to roll her eyes. She knew the propaganda bit. *The New United States. The nation this land was always meant to be. A new start. A new republic. One with all of the strengths of the old, but none of the weaknesses. A nation where every man, woman, and child has a place.*

Derek was already going on about it. "...and just imagine if no one was homeless, if no one went hungry, you know?" He focused on something invisible and far away. "Where you know what you're supposed to do, and everyone just does it. We all make it work, together. It's gonna be better, Lana, you just have to put your shoulder to the grindstone and remember that it's bigger than us, and..."

She kept looking at him, but his voice turned to noise in her ears. Derek was a true believer; she'd heard the talk before. She wished that she shared his optimism. But between her and any kind of hope for a better future, there was a wall that may as well have been a thousand miles high, every brick carved with her failures

She should have paid more attention, been a better shot, acted more decisively. If she hadn't fallen off that ledge, if she'd kicked harder, if she'd *been a better shot.*

If she'd done anything differently—even one little thing—Jessup might still be alive. Maybe she would have told him that she loved him. Maybe she *would* have loved him.

Now she'd never know. He died for her, *because* of her. And she had left him in the ash.

But that will never happen again. She stood and waved to the mat in front of her as Derek's speech trailed off. "Again. I need to get it right."

He tugged the knife from his belt as he rose. "Alright. So, just remember—twist, trap, hip. Then we'll work on the throw."

Derek attacked. Lana twisted, trapped, and slammed her hip into Derek's. Over and over and over. She worked until the movement was automatic. Until she didn't hesitate.

All the while, Jessup watched her, dying again, and again, and again.

CHAPTER THREE
CALEB

Horse Creek Base, New United States
Thursday, June 17th, 9:43 am EST

"Shopping list for Friday." Caleb read from the booklet he'd been given that morning into the radio receiver. "The kids are headed to the pool by noon. Pick up soda, white bread, pool noodles, transformer toys. Uncle John will be watching the kids. Aunt Mary has a cold. Over."

There was no response. There was never a response. But someone outside the base was listening. Obviously, it was some kind of code, but what it could possibly mean was beyond him. A reference to time, an event, possibly a contact. A supply drop of some kind?

If so, it was one of the more direct messages. Some of the transmissions were far more arcane in nature—from passages of fairy tales to strings of completely unrelated words. One message he'd read three days prior involved playing a cassette tape at specific intervals—an Aerosmith album, Nine Lives.

He'd been trying to figure out what he was actually doing; or, more specifically, what General Thomas was doing. As best he could tell, there were multiple operatives in the field, each with their own code scheme. If that was the case, it meant at least two things: no team was authorized to know what the others were doing, and the general was concerned operations might be observed.

All of it made him increasingly uncomfortable.

It had been a little over two weeks since he'd arrived at Horse Creek with his family. Two weeks since he first heard General Thomas say three words that turned Caleb's guts to ice. *New United States.* He'd half hoped the ice would thaw in time, but since he made repairs to the base's radio array and became the base's main comms officer, it had only grown harder, colder, and more jagged around the edges.

He glanced at his watch, waited another five minutes, then moved to the next message, adjusting the frequency and amplitude on the dials of the old machinery to the numbers listed by the text. "Little Red Riding Hood was walking in the forest, headed to her grandmother's house, when a wolf crossed her path..."

Could be a warning to a particular team—Red Riding Hood. Maybe it's a warning that they've been compromised or need to look out for something. Supply line?

Ruminating on what the messages might mean was compulsive, and made worse by the fact that he'd never intercepted a communication coming in. He'd scanned frequencies while unobserved, but he suspected his job was only to send the messages out. Private Carson likely worked the other half of the job taking down responses.

There were only a handful of reasons to keep the incoming and outgoing messages from ending up in the same place with the same person. None good.

General Thomas might be concerned about an intelligence leak, which meant the base could be compromised, and that was bad for everyone. On the other hand, controlling intelligence was a good way to keep one hand from knowing what the other was doing—only a small number of people saw the full picture. There were plenty of good reasons for that, but a lot of bad ones, too.

Once upon a time, Caleb had trusted his commanding officers, trusted the chain of command all the way to the top. Then the sky had fallen, and the government had downplayed it. He'd had to flee with his family, escaping the destruction that the chain of command had chosen to abandon half the United States to.

Maybe that had changed him, made him less trusting. Made him doubt whether the people in charge were really looking out for their people. But if anyone else in Horse Creek felt that way, he couldn't tell. For the most part, they all seemed to idolize General Thomas.

There was a knock at the door to the comms room, which was about three times the size of a closet. Caleb checked the time. His shift was over, the last of the messages conveyed. He closed the booklet and slid it off the console before standing and moving to the door to switch out with Private Carson.

Except, when he opened the door, it wasn't Carson on the other side. He frowned at the unfamiliar face of a young man with a corporal's patch on the chest of his fatigues, the name L. Masterson printed beneath it. The kid had a round face, and eyes that were just a little too far apart. His nose was crooked, broken badly in the past. His hand snapped up in a salute. "Staff Sergeant."

Caleb saluted in response. "At ease, Corporal. Where's Private Carson? He normally relieves me."

Corporal Masterson shook his head. "Can't say that I know, sir. I was just assigned."

Caleb glanced back at the comms station console, then looked Masterson over. "I had to train Carson myself. You know how to work the console?"

"Yes sir." Masterson peered past him. "All due respect, sir, my shift is meant to start in about three minutes."

"Right." Caleb quickly stepped aside to let the corporal into the room. Once he was past, a more familiar face greeted him, and he handed his booklet to Lieutenant Mackie, taking a clipboard from him in return.

Mackie was a burly guy, about Caleb's size, with the sort of face that could be mistaken for a pile of rocks if it was the right color. He rarely spoke, and always wore an expression like he was about to hit someone. Caleb tried to talk to him a few times, but never got much back and so just stopped trying. He signed, dated, and time stamped on the custody record for the book and handed the clip-board back without a word.

Mackie glanced over it, nodded, and then reached past Caleb to close the door to comms. "You are relieved, Staff Sergeant."

Caleb exchanged salutes and held his tongue when the instinct to ask about Carson arose. If Mackie knew anything, it was doubtful he would say. So he turned and left, keeping his posture and expression casually neutral.

It had taken him a few days to train Private Carson. After that, they'd only seen one another when they traded places. There was always a fifteen-minute gap between when Caleb finished and Carson started. That had been what made him think that Carson's job was to take down the responses; operatives in the field would have been told to listen for communications at a partic-ular time, then wait a specified length of time before responding.

The thing was, he'd asked Private Carson whether that was what he did during his shift. He'd asked him about it two days before, when he thought they were alone. Carson declined to answer, and Caleb let it go without argument.

Now, this Corporal arrived to take his place.

Coincidence, maybe. As far as Caleb knew, *he* wasn't being replaced. Then again, he was the only competent comms engineer on the base. Now that the comms were up and in good repair though, he could easily train someone to replace him. But the windstorms worsened recently, and there was no telling when the arrays on top of the base would need repairing. So he wasn't expendable.

The thought made him miss a step. Was Carson expendable?

Don't be paranoid. Carson got reassigned, that's all. It fits the pattern, keeping intelligence spread out so no one sees the whole picture. They just rotated him out, that's all. It isn't like there are enough people on base to...

To what? Disappear someone?

He shook the thought off. He'd see Carson at mess, probably.

When he reached his quarters, he half hoped to see Liz waiting for him, but she'd already left for mess duty apparently. He imagined Lana was out on janitorial.

He sighed as he tugged his boots off before sinking down onto Liz's cot, the metal creaking loudly in the small room. Her pillow smelled like her. Not like her shampoo, or whatever perfume she'd worn that day, the way her pillows used to smell. They didn't have anything like that on base, so when he breathed in the smell it was just *her*.

Lately, they hadn't seen enough of one another. Caleb started his shift in the comms room around three in the morning each day, and she started the breakfast shift at five. Sometimes, they'd gotten up around the same time and been able to grab a moment to themselves before they went to their duties. But Liz wasn't used to living on less than eight hours of sleep, so most mornings he did his best not to wake her.

Still, he saw more of his wife than he did his daughter. Lana spent her mornings training with PFC Derek Walker, her days on janitorial, and her nights avoiding Caleb. He'd been trying to give her space because Liz seemed to think she needed it. Time to process, to grieve, and to do those things in a place that didn't offer much of anything in the way of helping.

He worried for his family. They'd made it to safety. They were supposed to be together now but had been basically separated as soon as the opportunity arose.

Was there a reason for that? Part of some grand plan the general had in mind? A way of isolating anyone with connections to anything other than the general's big plans?

Paranoid thinking, sure.

But it was only paranoia if he was wrong. And he was starting to feel like maybe he *wasn't*.

The thing was, though... What the hell did they do if he was right?

CHAPTER FOUR
ELIZABETH

Horse Creek Base, New United States
Thursday, June 17th, 9:55 am EST

Elizabeth never imagined a day when she'd enjoy the smell of baked beans quite so much. Maple and brown sugar filled her nose, sweet and savory, triggering a memory of Lana's graduation party. A cookout with many of her friends and neighbors, Elizabeth decided to go all out and make a batch from scratch.

She'd soaked the beans overnight in salted water but forgot to rinse. One bite an hour before dinner and all she tasted was salt. In the end, she'd rushed to the store, brought back about ten cans, and heated them in a baking dish.

Caleb had told her how good they were, and said he was impressed. She'd let him be, and never told him they were store-bought. They'd been a hit with Lana's friends, too.

She glanced over at Marta—her third kitchen partner since she'd started mess duty—and smiled. "Never thought I'd appreciate a can of beans this much. If I never smell canned tamales again, it'll be too soon."

Marta was a narrow-faced woman, fine-boned, and pretty, with long dark hair that was probably always flowing and shiny before the meteor. Now, it was pulled back into a tail, like Elizabeth's own hair. She glanced up briefly, her eyes dropping to the can she held, and she nodded. "Yeah."

"I used to love these as a kid," Elizabeth went on as she poured the contents of the can into the big soup pot on the stove. "I thought beans with hotdog pieces in them were something special. Of course, then you grow up."

"True," Marta agreed without looking up from the frozen hamburger patties crumbling in her hands. Not exactly hotdog pieces, but it was the same principle, and it was what they had to work with this time around.

"Did you have something like that?" Elizabeth wondered, watching the woman.

Marta only shrugged. "Not really."

Three days she'd worked with Marta, and for three days Elizabeth had tried to start conversations. Anything at all—where she was from, what she'd done before the disaster, if she had family somewhere. Like the other two women, she seemed almost afraid to give more than a one-word answer to most questions.

Yes. No. Maybe. Not really. Sure. And that was when the answers were words instead of grunts of acknowledgment.

She'd had a therapist once, who'd said that if you keep having the same problem with people, then maybe the common denominator is *you*. She was starting to think there was something to that, and that her kitchen partners didn't want to talk to her because she was boring, or somehow upsetting.

But in fairness to Marta—and herself—it wasn't just the people Elizabeth worked with. And it hadn't just been her experience. Lana managed to make something of a friend, or maybe something more, with a young man who was teaching her self-defense, but other than that she'd found everyone on janitorial duty to be similarly tight-lipped. Caleb was uncomfortable talking about it, but seemed to be having the same experience.

No one on the base talked to them. No one on the base responded when they tried to start a conversation. The only time anyone said more than a few words at a time, was when they talked about the general.

And, frankly, Elizabeth was tired of hearing about the man as if he were some kind of hero. She dared not say it out loud, though. Not after seeing the way some of the soldiers acted around him.

The way they hung on his every word at meals, when he gave speeches about the good work they were doing and how everything was going to be better, greater, stronger. The country the United States was always meant to be. They cheered him when he gave those speeches. Elizabeth cheered as well, but not because she was moved. She was just afraid of what would happen if she didn't.

No one trusted her family. Not even enough to talk about their lives before all of this. It had begun to eat at her, gnawing away at her insides to make a hollow pit that kept whispering to her: *something is wrong here. This was a mistake.*

She thought it just then, as she watched Marta's flat expression, and the almost mechanical way she processed the frozen meat. Who didn't want to talk while they worked? What was *wrong* with the woman? For that matter, what had been wrong with Selena or Roxanne, the two other women who'd been rotated into mess duty with her? What made them so nervous to talk to her?

Elizabeth wasn't a soldier. What was she going to do with any information she gleaned from talking casually about their lives? Did they think she was a spy? And if so, a spy for *whom?* She'd seen the people outside.

If they were even still alive, somehow surviving the ash fall, and the windstorms that Caleb said had scraped parts of the mountainside down to the rock in places, and the violent earthquakes that had almost certainly devastated every building in hundreds of miles. Even if they were still out there, they weren't organized. They were just bandits and worse.

Caleb was a *marine*. She was a marine's wife; Lana was a marine's daughter. What was there to be so cautious about with them?

Not for the first time, she thought about leaving. About going to Caleb and telling him that she didn't feel safe, and that they shouldn't have come here. They could keep going west, see if there was some place out there where things were better. It was still summer, and even if it was getting colder, it wouldn't get deadly cold until the winter, surely. They could make it.

Unless they didn't.

And that was what stopped her every time. If it were just her and Caleb, she wouldn't have hesitated. But there was Lana to think about. They'd saved her. If it hadn't been the ash or the desperate people, it would have been the wind, or the ground falling out from beneath their feet at the wrong time that would have killed them.

Or worse, only taken Lana. Or Caleb. She didn't even know what was out there, what they might have to fight just to make it another day.

At least inside this hole in the mountain, they had something like security. Tenuous, sure, but a lot more predictable than anything the world outside might throw at them.

So, like all the other times she'd considered it, she pushed the thought away. They were doing this for Lana.

"Do you have kids?" she asked Marta.

"No."

"Guess it's probably better that way these days." Elizabeth opened the last can of beans. "One less thing to worry about."

"I guess," Marta replied.

Elizabeth shook the last of the beans out into the pot and adjusted the burner to a simmer. "That's the last of those. The boys must have found a grocery store or something. Wonder if they managed to bring back anything else."

Marta shrugged. "No telling."

"I'd kill for some tomatoes," Elizabeth mused. "I'd even settle for canned. And some pasta. I bet we could turn some of the beef patties into meatballs."

Marta gave a shallow nod but said nothing as she tapped a blunt knife between two more patties and shifted the frozen meat to the large pan to cook.

Alrighty then. Elizabeth had hit her limit of awkwardness for the day. She gathered up the empty cans and stripped them of their labels. Nothing was wasted here: cans were melted down, labels mulched for paper.

After a quick rinse, she deposited the cans and their labels into their respective containers, which were nearly full. "Are you fine finishing up? If so, I'll empty the cans for recycling."

Nothing. She wasn't even sure Marta heard her, but the kitchen wasn't loud, and she didn't whisper. *Maybe she's sick of me, too.*

With a sigh, Elizabeth shook her head and closed the lid on the trash bin before hauling it away from the wall. She turned it around, tipped it onto its wheels, and pulled it toward the kitchen's back door and into the hallway that ran down the base's south side.

We're doing this for Lana. If it means being uncomfortable for a while, it's not like I've never had to keep my head down.

She pulled the trashcan along the hallway, turned left

at the end, and pushed through a pair of double doors into the part of the complex housing the recycling area.

Halfway through the doors, a familiar voice caught her ear, and she froze. It was the general, his voice low and clipped.

"...telling me they got the jump on you, Lieutenant?"

He sounded angry. She started to back away, to go back through the doors. This didn't sound like something she was supposed to hear. But the next words froze her in place again.

"Our intel was inaccurate, sir." A man's voice she didn't recognize. "And, sir, it came from Machert. If I didn't know better, I'd say he set us up."

CHAPTER FIVE
ELIZABETH

Horse Creek Base, New United States
Thursday, June 17th, 10:14 am EST

Elizabeth's legs stiffened like pillars of concrete in the middle of the hall. Stomach twisting with sudden nausea, she covered her mouth with a shaky hand. This stranger blamed Caleb for, what, ambush? *Impossible.* And what intel? Caleb barely left the base, and then only to repair radio equipment. Or at least, that's what he told her.

General Thomas's next words eased her rising surge of terror. "Lieutenant, were you led to believe that Staff Sergeant Machert is all-knowing? Or that he has been endowed with some supernatural prescience that allows him to see the future? Has someone told you that he's a prophet?"

The Lieutenant stammered his response. "N-no, sir, but—sorry, sir. I just meant—"

"You meant," the general interrupted, "that you

received intel about insurgents, acted rashly on the intel, and operated counter to what were very clear instructions regarding the nature of your mission. You were to observe, confirm, update base, and await orders, Lieutenant. Is that what you did?"

Insurgents? Elizabeth's brow pinched. How could there be an insurgency? There were dangerous people out there, certainly, but they were just people.

"No, sir," the Lieutenant admitted. "We were spotted, and it became necessary to take action immediately."

Blood sloshed through her ears like water through a full open faucet in the long pause that followed. Elizabeth clamped her hand tighter across her mouth, worried her labored breathing and pounding heart would draw unwanted attention. The whooshing in her ears only grew louder.

"What's your assessment, then, Lieutenant?" the general asked, his voice calmer. Did that mean Caleb wasn't in trouble? That the general didn't suspect him of being a traitor?

The Lieutenant's reply was more clipped now. "With the weather changing, there's a lot more traffic, General. Now the ash is out of the air, mostly, and a few good rains have made it easier to breathe, we're seeing more locals moving through the mountains. Sometimes in small groups, sometimes in large ones. By and large, they're unarmed and no trouble for us, but lately we're seeing more and more weapons. Even when it's just a few."

"This group that got the drop on you?" General Thomas asked. "Composition?"

"Primarily civilians. Three armed men, possibly family members, but not clear. Far as we can tell, they were headed our direction, but indirectly. I don't think they had our location, but that makes the sixth group we've found headed our way. Someone knows we're up here, and I think we're seeing more armed locals—"

"Insurgents," the general corrected.

"—*insurgents*, sir," the lieutenant covered quickly. "I think we're seeing more armed because they know other people have come this way and disappeared. We're over thirty bodies, and most of those in the last six days. Best guess, they're coming from farther and farther away, and clustering together as they make it here from the coastal areas. The ones we've managed to question all have pretty much the same story."

Elizabeth pressed her hand tighter to her mouth and swallowed down the wave of half-digested oatmeal rising in the back of her throat. Thirty *bodies*? They'd encountered some awful people when they fled Greensboro, but that was a good-sized city. Not the side of a mountain on the outskirts of a tiny town.

The lieutenant continued. "We've been looking for people with the kind of skills we need, sir, the problem is, they usually come attached to people who don't. So far, we've only recruited two who were willing to leave their people behind, and neither of those worked out. I'm not arguing with your standing orders, but if we changed tact—"

"Let me tell you what happens if we change tactics, Lieutenant." The general's voice took on a hard edge.

"For every ten basically worthless civilians we give shelter to, we get one solid serviceman who still has to be properly trained and broken in. That's eleven mouths to feed and only one of them is barely pulling their weight. We can't rebuild this country with a bunch of needy welfare-seeking civvies who are too used to being coddled and who've spent their entire lives looking to people like us to do the hard work. Those days are over, and they aren't coming back."

"O—of course, sir," the lieutenant stammered. "I suppose that what I mean is that it may not be an ideal strategy. As long as we're hidden here, we're an unknown factor. If we were able to put out a call, though—to execute a proper recruitment drive—we might have better luck bolstering our ranks."

The general scoffed, followed quickly by the clipped tapping of boot heels on concrete. The sound grew louder, and Elizabeth took an involuntary step back. Her shoulder nudged the recycling bin and it rocked backward before momentum carried it forward. She caught it just before the wheels struck the floor and carefully lowered it back.

The footsteps stopped and General Thomas's voice sounded dangerously close. "I'm not completely turned off by the idea. But it's not something I'm willing to do lightly, either. Right now, our comms aren't much more sophisticated than what the civilians have. That'll change soon, though. When it does, we'll be able to keep our operations better classified, secure the area, and keep a border. Maybe then, I'll consider a public recruitment drive. Until then, carry on. Make everyone who seems worth it the offer. The ones who don't—put them out of their misery. We can't take on the dead weight, and they'll just be a nuisance down the line."

"Sir." The word was accompanied by a sharp snap of fabric and the impact of two boot heels against one another—a sound that Elizabeth heard dozens of times a day when one of the general's men saluted.

"Dismissed, Lieutenant," the general said. "And keep your mistrust of Staff Sergeant Machert to yourself. I'll have a talk with him and see for myself, but for the moment we need him. Unless you pick up another comms engineer in the wild, understood?"

"Understood, Sir."

After that, the footsteps resumed in two sets—one receding, and one headed her way. Elizabeth bit her lip hard to keep from cursing, then looked frantically around her. There was no place to hide, and if she ran, she would be spotted, questioned—and she was a terrible liar.

Instead, she rushed to the door and pulled it open before letting it swing shut as she pulled the bin ahead of her. The door closed with a heavy thud just as General Thomas turned a corner.

He stopped when he saw her, and Elizabeth felt her face pale. Fortunately, so did most of the civilian staff when the general glowered. She dipped her head. "General Thomas. Good to see you, sir."

"Missus Machert," he replied with a nod. He peered at the bin, and at the door.

She glanced back at the bin, then lifted the lid.

"Cans. Taking them to be recycled. It's chili for lunch. We... hit critical mass with the supplies. It'll be a nice break from MREs, I hope."

"A break from MREs is always welcomed," he agreed. "Carry on. Give your girl my regards. I hear she's got her eye on enlistment."

Elizabeth knew that was the case and had already tried to talk Lana out of it. Now, though, she had a sudden flash of Lana in the field, with some unit, pointing a gun at civilians. Pulling the trigger because none of them looked like they could carry their own weight.

"Everything alright, Missus Machert?" General Thomas asked, head tipped in question.

"Yes." The word wobbled on her tongue, and she wiped sweat from her forehead. "Everything is... great. If you'll excuse me, I need to empty this out and get back to the kitchen. I hate to, ah—there's not really space to go around you, sir."

It was true, and fortunately so, because the general glanced around himself and then gave her a friendly smile as he stepped aside, nearly pressed against the wall. "There you go. You'll have to forgive me—I'm not used to moving for anyone."

No, Elizabeth didn't imagine he was. She slipped past him with a forced smile. "I'll tell Lana you said hello. She's... uh, she's looking forward to it. To enlisting, I mean. She'd be honored. Thank you, General. I hope you enjoy the chili."

Stop talking, you idiot! she chided herself as she finally tore her eyes from the man and double-timed it to the recycling hub at the end of the hallway. The general didn't call out to her, didn't tell her to stop and explain whether she'd heard anything she shouldn't have. Didn't spring any of the surprises she instinctively expected from the man; or at least, men like him.

Because she did know men like him. Men who thought like him, anyway. Men with power, or resources, or anything someone might need, who believed they had a right to decide who had sufficient value to exchange for it.

Her mother's parade of abusive boyfriends and hook-ups had been exactly like that. Drunk with what little power they were able to squeeze out of whoever would let them take it, grinding down everyone in sight just to make themselves feel like a king that everyone bowed and scraped for, hoping for the smallest crumb of dignity and acknowledgment.

It never lasted though, and no amount of bowing and scraping was ever enough to make a person like that experience one second of remorse for what they'd done or to even see other people as human beings at all. Any peace with a person like that was temporary.

And when it was over, there was always bloodshed.

CHAPTER SIX
CALEB

Horse Creek Base, New United States
Thursday, June 17th, 12:47 pm EST

Something's wrong. Caleb eyed his wife across the mess over lunch. She'd barely looked at him when he came through the mess line and accepted a bowl of chili. Her eyes flicked up at him furtively as she ladled the chow, then back down to her work. Now she ignored him completely, head down, eyes focused on the job. Unusual to say the least.

Seeing one another, even briefly during the day, had been a moment of relief since their details had put them on mostly opposite schedules. A reminder that they would have a few hours together at night to look forward to.

This, though—a nervous meeting of his eyes and a white-knuckle grip on the ladle, her fingers fidgeting on the edge of her apron—this was fear. But of what?

He finished his meal, running through the possibilities over and over, before hurrying through equipment inventory reports. Before his equipment checks began on the outside of the base, he detoured to their room, imagination getting the better of him.

Maybe the new woman assigned to help in the kitchen was mean or rude. Maybe she was disappointed with the food supply. Please let it be that. And not a version of the worries keeping him awake at night. The ones leading him down a path that would be dangerous for his family.

He pushed the door open, and Elizabeth was already waiting for him, same as she was most days for the little half-hour window in the early afternoon. "Hey." He kept his voice low as he closed the door behind him. "What's going on? You looked scared half to—"

She stood from the bed, wringing her hands as she took a nervous step toward him, her eyes on the door over his shoulder before she looked up into his troubled expression, the wide-eyed fear evident on her face. "Caleb... we can't stay here."

Caleb's mouth opened, then closed as he curbed his initial reaction, which was to say she needed to calm down. She'd always hated it when he told her that. And given what he'd had on his mind the last few days...

"Alright," he said after a moment. "What's going on? What happened?"

Elizabeth took a slow, shaky breath in before she told him about the incident in the hallway. At first, it didn't make any sense even though he did believe her. "Why would they have this discussion in the hall?"

"It's out of the way," Elizabeth explained. "I've never seen anyone else in it when I go to the recycling. Maybe they didn't think anyone would be there."

"Or they didn't think it needed to be a privileged conversation," Caleb pointed out.

Her eyes narrowed at him. "You mean maybe it wasn't all that serious and I'm blowing it out of proportion."

That hadn't been his intention, but he put his hands up anyway. "I'm just getting the full picture. A mission debrief shouldn't have been taking place in the open if it was this sensitive, that's all. So... maybe it was urgent?"

Liz's jaw tightened. "They are *killing* people, Caleb. And the lieutenant tried to throw you under the bus."

That *was* alarming, but it sounded like the general hadn't taken the bait. Still, it would be good to know who was trying to put Caleb in the line of fire. "You remember the lieutenant's name?"

She shook her head as she stepped toward the cot and dropped down to the edge of it. "Thomas just called him by his rank. I think I've heard his voice, but I couldn't tell you who it belongs to."

There were four Lieutenants in the building. Caleb knew Lieutenant Richard Davis personally, but the other three he'd only met in passing. He wouldn't have called Davis a friend, exactly, but he doubted he'd have blamed a failed reconnaissance mission on anyone else; he seemed like the sort of man who took responsibility for his missions. Though, maybe Caleb overestimated him. All four had a much longer relationship with the general than Caleb did, and he had no idea what the dynamics of those relationships were.

It didn't exactly leave anyone he could trust to find out more. "Did they mention a region? A sector, they might have said."

Elizabeth shook her head again. "But does it even matter? *Thirty* people have been killed. The general doesn't want 'unskilled' civilians here, and he's got a standing order to execute them. That's enough for us to need to *leave* this place, isn't it?"

Caleb's mind flashed to the people they'd encountered on the way up the mountain. Unskilled didn't mean innocent. *But I already have a bad feeling,* he admitted to himself. *Why am I so intent on trying to find a way to overlook Thomas's actions?*

It was a good question, and probably the right one to be asking. But the answer was easy enough to recognize. "If we leave here, Liz," he offered gently, "I don't know where we'll go."

"*Anywhere else,*" she hissed at him. "Caleb, if we stay here, how long before you're asked to kill someone just because that man says they're unworthy to *live*? How long before Lana enlists, and must make that same choice? Or before... before Thomas decides that you're the only 'useful' member of this family? I'm terrified. For me, for Lana—and for you, because I *know* what choice you'll make if he asks you to."

He was at least reassured by that. Liz knew that he'd

never hurt her, or Lana. And that he'd never gun down an unarmed civilian just looking for safety. But she did have a point.

There would be swift and likely fatal consequences for all of them if he refused an order. Caleb hadn't *seen* the general order a soldier executed for disobeying orders, but there had been casualties in the field—and some of them seemed unlikely to be at the hands of civilian groups Caleb had overheard on the radio.

"You're right," he admitted, finally. "We might be in danger here, even if it's not immediate. But the best thing we can do right now, is play along, learn more, and find... I don't know, find the right way out. If we take a wrong step here, we'll—"

The door opened. Caleb's heart leaped into his throat, his body tensing as he turned reflexively to the door, hands already coming up defensively as adrenaline pumped into his system.

He exhaled a sharp breath when he saw Lana in the doorway. His shoulders relaxed, but a different kind of tension filled his stomach when his daughter's eyes narrowed. "What do you mean, 'way out'? What's going on?"

Caleb waved a hand to dismiss the question. "Nothing, honey. Nothing you have to worry about, we're just talking."

That was the wrong thing to say, and he probably could have guessed as much if he'd taken the time to think before he said it. Lana's back went rigid. "If something's going on," she said, her voice icy, "then I have a right to know. You're talking about leaving, aren't you? What did you mean by 'wrong step'? Are we in trouble? Did you do something?"

"Lana, no," Caleb told her, "we're not in trouble, we're just... your mom and I have some things to talk about, that's all. You've got too much going on to worry about our problems."

"Too much going on," Lana echoed, and folded her arms over her chest as she eyed first him, then Liz, then focused a sharp look on him, meeting his eyes with an unflinching gaze. "I'm not the kid who left for college, Dad. Not anymore."

A look crossed her face. One that Caleb knew and had seen on her before—and on the faces of combat veterans. It was brief, as if she pushed it away; as if she'd been getting practice doing so. A look of haunted pain that unfocused her eyes and paled her cheeks. She swallowed and she was back.

"Lana," Caleb murmured, "honey, I know you're not—"

"Caleb, stop," Elizabeth interrupted, standing from the cot to put a hand on his arm. "She needs to know."

Before he could slow things down, Elizabeth blurted it all out. Caleb's chest tightened. He wanted to protect his daughter, not put her in harm's way. If she knew about the general's plans, she would be a liability. A security risk.

As Elizabeth finished, she smiled a sad, conciliatory smile at their daughter. "I'm sorry. Hon. But the general is out of his mind, and this place isn't safe for us. And even if it was... we couldn't be a part of that. We can't stay here."

Lana didn't look furious, or afraid. She looked... offended, maybe? Caleb reached out for her. "We're not leaving right away—"

His daughter jerked backward, away from his touch, her face twisting with anger that made her next words come out ragged and harsh. "So, what, then?" Her eyes welled with sudden tears. "Everything we went through meant nothing? We made a *mistake*? I let Jessup get killed and it's just *Whoops, we're in the wrong place*?"

Elizabeth's hand tightened on Caleb's arm, her nails digging into his skin. "Lana—what?"

Caleb's heart broke. That's what he'd seen on her face a moment before, then. *Guilt.*

"Honey, you didn't *let* Jessup die. That wasn't your fault, you must believe that. It was dangerous out there— those men that attacked us... *they* killed Jessup, baby girl."

"Don't *call* me that," she growled, and wiped her eyes as she took another step toward the door. "I'm not a *baby*. Or a *girl*; I'm a grown woman and I... I *know* what happened."

"Of course you aren't," Caleb said, and started to reach for her again. "Lana, please, let's just—"

But she threw her hands up and took another step back before turning and stalking away. Caleb moved to follow, but Elizabeth's grip on him tightened again and she pulled him back. "Caleb, don't. She needs space."

"She needs someone to explain that what happened to Jessup wasn't her fault," he replied as he tried to gently remove his wife's hand from his arm. "I've seen that kind of survivor's guilt before, I know what it looks like, I can bring her around."

"And what," Elizabeth demanded with equal gentleness. "You'll fix it for her?"

His jaw clenched as fresh guilt twisted in his gut, made worse by the sense of helplessness that clawed at his heart. He relaxed under Liz's grip, and she eased up on him before she put a hand to his cheek, her eyes misty and soft.

"I'm worried about her too. But right now, she's processing something awful. Or maybe *not* processing it. Either way, it's not something you can just step in and fix, Caleb. She didn't get a fishing line tangled, or set a tent up wrong, or even break a leg. Just take a minute to think about what you'd even say."

Again, Liz was right. That was exactly what he wanted—to go to Lana, tell her it wasn't her fault, and make her believe it. As if that would somehow override whatever trauma was in her now, telling her lies and changing her, changing how she saw herself and the world.

That wasn't something he could fix. There was no bolt to tighten, nothing to untangle. Nothing he could just step in and reassure her about—that he was there, that she was his daughter, his little girl, and that daddy was there for her to keep her safe.

She *wasn't* safe. And it was possible, now, that he couldn't keep her safe. Just like he couldn't keep Elizabeth safe. Not now, not in this. Not when the predictable order of the world before the disaster had been thrown into chaos.

The thought of that terrified him. *I can't keep them safe.*

His eyes burned, but he refused to let the thought consume him. Maybe he couldn't personally, physically, always keep them both safe. But he could at least work on making sure there were fewer threats.

"You're right," he said softly, and bent his neck to kiss Liz, soaking up the brief reassurance that she was there, that he still had her; that he hadn't lost anything truly valuable to him *yet*. "We can't stay here forever."

She looked up at him. "Then what do we do?" she asked, searching his eyes. "I've known men like General Thomas. He's got his hands on a little power, made his little kingdom here, and he's not going to let it go. We're only safe as long as we're willing to play along, follow his rules, his orders. He'll test you, Caleb. He'll test all of us, that's what this kind of man does."

Caleb knew the type as well, but not the same way Elizabeth did. He didn't have her history. She was right, though; he could feel it in his gut. If General Thomas had any reason at all to suspect Caleb or his family didn't belong in his New United States, he'd test them, push them to the limits of their loyalty.

When he did, would Caleb fail? Even if it meant putting his family in danger? Could he 'play along' if it meant becoming someone who didn't even deserve them?

If it meant he could be sure they were safe, probably. If it meant that Elizabeth looked at him and saw the kinds of monsters Caleb had tried so hard to save her from...

No.

"I'm not sure yet." He smoothed a lock of hair behind her ear, gratified at the way her eyes relaxed and she leaned against his fingers. He wasn't a monster yet, at least. Not to her.

"But I will figure it out. In the meantime, keep your head down." He glanced at the watch on his wrist. His time was up. "Look, I have to do my maintenance round outside. After, I'll find Lana and make sure she understands and... give her the chance to open up, if she's ready."

At that, Elizabeth withdrew. "You should. She's more likely to talk to you than me."

She didn't mean to stab him, but he felt the words cut into him all the same. "No, I didn't mean... I'm sorry, Liz, I just meant that I know where she'll be and..."

If he kept talking, he would almost certainly make it worse and he was late. The last thing he needed was to call attention to himself by failing to keep his duty schedule. "I have to go. I'll see you tonight. Remember what I said, please—keep out of harm's way for now. I promise, I'll figure it out, I'll..."

He let his words die. *I'll fix this,* he was going to say. Elizabeth glanced up at him with a sad smile, and he suspected that she'd heard the unspoken words anyway. She gave him a nod. "I'll see you tonight," she agreed. "I love you, Caleb."

"I love you." He kissed the top of her head before he

forced himself to leave. As much as he hated it, Elizabeth knew *how* to keep her head down. She'd had to do it before.

Lana, on the other hand, hadn't. Once upon a time, Caleb had been proud of that.

Now, it just terrified him.

Horse Creek Base, New United States
Thursday, June 17th, 4:33 pm EST

Elizabeth's words rang in Caleb's ears throughout his repairs. *We're only safe here if we're willing to give up who we are.*

Given what they'd seen and heard the last two weeks, he couldn't deny that she was at least partially right. General Thomas demanded more than just competence from his people, more than just a willingness to follow orders and trust the chain of command. He wanted devotion, loyalty, even zeal for the promise of this New United States.

And honestly, the ideals he preached were worth investing in. Maybe that was why it had been so easy to overlook the culture that pervaded the base. In a time of crisis, people looked to leaders and clung to hope. Military personnel weren't immune to their own basic human nature.

He tightened the final bolt of a reinforcing brace for one of the radio arrays and leaned back on his heels. *I'm not even immune to it. I'd give almost anything to live somewhere Liz and Lana could be safe and even thrive.*

But now that Elizabeth had given that price a name, put a dollar sign next to it... was it true? If they gave up who they were—if he set aside his morals and his most basic beliefs—then what would they have left afterward? He wouldn't be the man that Liz had married, or the father that Lana had looked up to. He'd be someone different. They would be different.

Lana already was, maybe.

He gave the array a tug, testing the reinforcement. The rattle was gone, but the wind wasn't blowing with deadly force like before. Whether the array could stand up to real pressure, he'd just have to find out.

Not that different from us. He slipped the wrench back into his toolbelt and began the descent. *Easy to say we know who we are until there's real pressure and we're forced to find out.*

But when the pressure was on, would they all bend the same direction? Elizabeth clearly didn't believe this was a place they could stay, or something they could be a part of. Caleb was inclined to agree, but still wanted to know more. Lana's position wasn't at all clear to him.

She'd sacrificed to get here. They all had, but Lana lost someone who probably meant more to her than she'd realized. Or maybe it was just the fact that she'd lost someone to violence for the first time.

She'd been lucky most of her life when it came to grief. Caleb's parents had died when she was too young to really feel the loss, and Elizabeth's parents had never been in the picture. Their family had always been small. Lana had never lost a friend or loved one. She hadn't had to grieve or cope before.

Military life was enticing when a person was grieving. There was purpose and structure in it. Clear goals, clear rewards, clear consequences, even clear ways to make yourself better. She wanted to be a soldier, to feel competent and safe. She wanted to know that just because she lost someone, it didn't mean that everything could slip through her fingers any second.

All of that, Caleb understood. He saw it clearly.

What he couldn't see almost at all, was whether his daughter was on the verge of committing to the kind of extremism favored by General Thomas.

By the time he was back on the ground, his radio clicked twice, and a voice came over. "Staff Sergeant Machert." Private Vance Kidder's voice crackled. "Report to General Thomas in the ready room, ASAP. Over."

A chill passed through Caleb's gut. After what Elizabeth overheard, he'd been wondering if Thomas would demand an explanation for Caleb's perceived sabotage of an operation. Truth be told, he was surprised it had taken this long. He plucked the radio from his belt. "Acknowledged, Private. On route. Over."

Kidder didn't respond and didn't need to. Caleb put the radio back in place and made his way to the front of the base's entrance. The two guards stationed there gave him a curt salute when he appeared and one of them swiped a card over the lock pad to let him in.

Once inside, he didn't bother to put his equipment away. ASAP ostensibly meant 'as soon as possible', but the reality was that it meant 'right now' in almost every context he'd encountered on base. Plus, having his kit on *might* just make for a visual reminder that he wasn't as expendable here as a lot of the unskilled grunts. If he was right about what the general wanted, it wouldn't be a bad idea to have that reminder on hand.

He stepped off the elevator down into the base's guts and then made his way to Thomas's ready room. As he went, he found himself making more detailed notes than he had before. One guard at the armory, two other men inside doing inventory.

It was around three in the afternoon. Was inventory always at three? The supply room was manned by the quartermaster and three privates. Was there a shift change there, and if so what time?

Before, he'd been relieved to have his family behind solid walls and surrounded by armed soldiers. Safe from everything outside. Now, the place didn't feel safe. It felt like a trap that hadn't quite sprung. He was already thinking about what would be necessary to get his family out.

Outside Thomas's ready room, Sergeant Mackie was seated at a narrow desk. He looked up at Caleb, gave a nod and then tilted his head toward the door as he reached beneath the edge of his desk and pressed something. The door buzzed, and Caleb went through it.

The general was alone inside. He sat at his desk, paging through some printed report that he closed and laid down when the door closed behind Caleb. Caleb stood at attention, snapping a sharp salute as his eyes took in the wooden crate to one side of the desk. "General, sir. You requested me?"

General Thomas gave a nod and waved at the space in front of his desk. "I did, Staff Sergeant. At ease."

Caleb took the invitation and relaxed, moving to stand opposite the general, hands clasped behind his back, feet spread to shoulder-width as he waited.

The general nodded to the crate. "These have been kicking around storage. Any chance you've worked with them before?"

Assuming he was being asked to look, Caleb left at-ease and shifted the lid off the crate to look inside. Army-green plastic cases filled the crate, one of them open to display a row of four blocky radio units and a mobile comms box. He knew the model, but it had been out of date when he retired.

"Secure field comms. I'm familiar, sir, but haven't worked on them myself."

"Familiarity is a good start." General Thomas nodded at the crate. "Can you secure them properly without a sat connection?"

Caleb frowned down at the units. The system was simple enough, if he recalled any of the details correctly, but without a satellite uplink, they were fairly short range. It had been a long time since the US military had a need to secure short-wave transmissions. Sat-comms had made the technology just about obsolete.

"Can I ask the nature of the operation, sir?" Caleb asked, then quickly added, "I can absolutely get the radios secure, but it would be helpful to know what kind of capability you need. I'll have to hack it together, and I don't know that I can get you military-grade security quickly, but I could get you something working that your average civilian won't be able to crack."

General Thomas gave a thoughtful nod, but no direct answer. Instead, he said, "Lieutenant Warren voiced a concern recently about some intelligence you provided his unit. Communications between two insurgent groups from three days ago."

Although Caleb knew what the general meant, he shook his head. "Forgive me, sir, but you may have to be more specific. I've filed about a dozen intelligence reports in the last three days and don't always know where they end up."

"Chatter about two groups coordinating a scouting operation up the mountain," the general said, his expression still placid, no threat of warning in his tone. "I believe the report suggested there were six civilians in the scout group, unarmed?"

Caleb did know the report. The group had been using commercial grade radios to call in updates on their position, and he'd come across the communications as part of a routine radio surveillance check.

Most of those discoveries were essentially coincidence; it was impossible to monitor all frequencies on a constant basis with the equipment available on base. He had to manually check them during surveillance shifts and sometimes between transmissions in the mornings. This was the intelligence Elizabeth had overheard the comment about—that he'd given the lieutenant's unit bad intel intentionally.

Caleb knew the answer he gave would determine the consequences for what happened. He trod carefully. "I know the report, sir. Six civilians in all, and they'd relayed concern about being unarmed in the field. Worried mostly about some other group who'd been trouble in the past. If I recall, I reported that they were told to cover their area and then report back the following day. I marked it priority level four."

Thomas gave a shallow nod. "You did," he agreed. "I sent Lieutenant Warren's unit out to patrol the area, and they encountered the group. There were eight, in reality, and they were not unarmed."

Caleb's surprised reaction was genuine. He hadn't lied about what he'd heard. Whether the general believed him or not, though, was only half the problem with that. "Sir," he said carefully, "I can assure you that I relayed an accurate report of what I encountered. If the intelligence was wrong—"

"Relax, Staff Sergeant. I don't think you sabotaged your fellow soldiers. I'm more concerned that this group knew there was a possibility they were being overheard."

That was Caleb's concern as well. "Permission to speak freely, sir?"

Thomas waved him on. "Speak."

"If this group employed an intentional subterfuge tactic based on the assumption that their comms were compromised, the most likely reason is that they know the base is here, and at least suspect that it's occupied and operational. Or, they didn't know for certain but needed to find out. If Lieutenant Warren—"

Caleb caught himself before mentioning the aftermath; he wasn't supposed to know. He covered his hesitation by clearing his throat. "Pardon me, sir; I was just outside and still have a scratch in my throat. If the lieutenant made contact with this group, it might have confirmed intelligence they were hoping to gather."

"He did." The general leaned back in his chair. "There were no survivors. Which doesn't mean their fellow insurgents learned nothing, but it does mean they didn't learn anything specific. But we can't afford to let this problem go unchecked. Hence, I need the field comms. We need to clear the insurgents, secure this mountain, and establish a border. We have to operate under the assumption of a hostile force."

Clear the insurgents. Caleb weighed those words, and the next ones he spoke. Even if it lessened the general's trust in him, he couldn't stand by and say nothing. "Sir, are you certain these civilians... you're talking about killing Americans, sir. There are very likely small groups out there in competition against one another over resources, but if they knew there was leadership here, that there's a peacekeeping force in place—"

"I wasn't asking for your opinion, Staff Sergeant." He stood, and strode around the end of the desk, eyes searching Caleb's face. "You and your family were out there when this all came down. You've seen what happened, how people fell apart and gave in to their animal natures. Civilization vanished in an instant."

He shook his head in disgust. "These people believe they've been abandoned, Machert, and they're not wrong. We're going to give them back what they lost, but that can only happen once we've secured a proper foothold and shown them that we are the guiding force in this region. We must act decisively; show everyone we are not to be trifled with, and that there *is* still law and order in this country."

"By killing civilians, sir?" Caleb pressed, even knowing that he was treading on dangerous ground. "There has to be another way."

General Thomas put a hand on his shoulder. "There is. But between us and that path, are obstructions. Remove those, and we can change position and bring safety and civility back to these people. We're building a new nation here, Machert. The kind of place where Lana and Elizabeth will be safe. Protected. A land of plenty— of clarity, and purity of purpose."

He held out his free hand as if he were waving it over a horizon. "Once that wheat is sown, we can harvest it. But before we can even begin planting, the field must burn. Too much of the old is still poisoning this land.

This individualistic, self-serving culture that we allowed to grow in our country is going to be the end of us if we don't. Anything we try to grow from that soil is going to be poisoned in the same way. It's time for a *new* future, Machert. Are you and your family going to be a part of it?"

Unspoken was the other half of that question. *Are you going to be a part of it, or* not?

Caleb heard the silent part loud and clear. There was only one possible answer to give. "Of course we will, sir. You can count on me."

"I know I can." He squeezed Caleb's shoulder and then withdrew, returning to his desk. "Let supply know what you need to get these units working and secure. Commercial grade, as tight as you can get it, for now. I'll have the units delivered to engineering within the hour. The sooner the better, Staff Sergeant. We're losing ground every day we're not gaining it."

"Yes, sir."

"Dismissed."

Caleb saluted and left, his mind racing as he made his way to the engineering station. Military-grade security on the radio units would take time. That was good. He needed to buy as much time as he could.

No matter what he told the general, there was no way that he or his family could take part in the wholesale slaughter of civilians, or even let it happen. He might not have sabotaged a unit before, but he might have to, now.

He could rig the radios to fail, maybe, or... implement the encryption incompletely—nothing too obvious, but enough for anyone coming this direction to pick up on minimal chatter. The last thing he wanted was for soldiers who were just following orders to die. Some of them were good men; a lot of them were. He had to find a way to split the difference.

If he didn't, hundreds of people just trying to survive were going to die because of him.

Bartow Hill Road, Lansing, NC
Thursday, June 17th, 4:52 pm EST

Crunch. Crunch-crunch. Maddox lifted a sticky hand up to Lerlaine, nudging a Cheerio toward her mouth.

"No, baby." Lerlaine forced a smile. "Mama's fine." She didn't tell him this was the next-to-last box or explain how the dread coiling in her stomach made her nauseous and dizzy.

She ran a hand over his soft hair and down his back, her palm registering every bump of vertebrae in his spine. He squatted on the bed beside her, picking one bite of cereal at a time from his hand to first examine and then eat.

Hunter slept beside her, tucked against her hip after she finally managed to breastfeed him again. It had taken a few days of regular meals to make milk consistently, and she'd worried it had been too long until finally, she felt the swelling pressure and nearly broke down from relief. Ray, of course, hadn't stocked any formula.

But her children were fed. She was fed.

She reached up and fingered the tender bruise on her cheek. She'd asked Ray if they could drive down to Jackson, check the grocery store there for formula. Even one can would help supplement, at least, until she was back to full strength.

"Already been there," he'd told her.

"Did you look for formula, though?"

A reasonable question. They weren't living there anymore. Ray wouldn't think to look.

But he hadn't seen it that way. Just like before, she felt his anger before she saw it. It rippled through him invisibly, quieting the kitchen, filling the air with electric tension pricking her skin.

"No, Lerlaine." His voice remained soft and deadly. "I didn't look for formula, but you're not the only whore in the valley who got herself knocked up, you stupid f—"

The rest had been lost in the strange fog she always slipped into right before it happened. She never remembered the middle, and sometimes not even the end. Just the beginning. And the reminders that stuck with her for days or even weeks afterward. The bruises, the sore throat, worse.

She pulled her fingers away from the purpling skin and closed her eyes. From the living room, one of Ray's buddies raised his voice and drew her attention. She leaned over to catch a glimpse through the open door.

"There's just the four patrols, Henley, don't be a wimp!" Ryder, a compact bear of a man who'd known Ray since they were kids, accented his statement with a string of choice curse words.

Henley. Lerlaine thought back. Last time she'd heard his name, a prison sentence had been attached. Drugs, was it? Robbery?

Six other men crammed into the living room, amplifying the stench of body odor and stale dip juice to the point it soured Lerlaine's stomach. Nine men in total. She didn't know all of them, but based on their familiarity with the place, she guessed they were neighbors, men holed up in the hills like Ray.

She strained to hear, ears sharpened by the word *patrols. Patrols of what?*

"Jake said he *thinks* there's four." Henley tipped the chair he'd dragged in from the dining room back and added a few curse words for emphasis. "Can't nobody get close 'nough t'be sure. Folks go up there and don't come back, these ain't some redneck crackheads, you dumb SOB. They're some kinda military pricks with M4s. I'm tellin' ya, they execute anybody that gets close."

Ray barked out a curse. "I ain't scared by some boys sportin' military rifles. We got guns, too. Look," Ray leaned forward, elbows on his knees. "Jake says these pretty boys come by the ridge twice a day. So I'm thinkin' we set up right there on the hillside and pick 'em off one-by-one."

"Then what?"

Ray smiled and flecks of dip coated his teeth. "We

grab all their gear, then hit the next patrol that comes lookin'."

Lerlaine pulled her sleeves down to cover her knuckles. For the last two days, Ray had been non-stop about this compound, some military fort up on the mountain. Claimed it was full of food and weapons and all sorts of supplies.

"Jake's no dummy." A man Lerlaine didn't know waved in the direction of the mountain, bushy mustache twitching as he spoke. "If he says nobody comes back alive, then it ain't worth it, no matter how much they got holed up in there."

Ray argued some more, minimizing the risk between slugs of beer. Lerlaine swallowed down the acid inching up her throat. Ray wanted to ambush the military? He was drunk, sure, but being drunk didn't usually make him *that* reckless.

"They got radios and comm crap, Ray," someone said. "Even if we take out one patrol, the other three are gonna hear about it, or hear the shots. We can't do 'em one at a time."

"Then we go round up Cutter and Scoot." Ray pointed at each man as he counted. "That'll give us four groups of... well, three groups of three and one group of two. Where's Meatball? He still here or did he run off like a sissy the first sign of trouble?"

"Meat died," someone reported. "Got hit by one of them rocks at his camp up by the creek. Place got flattened. Burned. Probably buried under a hundred trees and ash."

Ray blew out a curse. "To Meatball." He raised his beer and drank.

"To Meatball," the others replied.

"Doesn't change anything." Ray nodded at a man Lerlaine couldn't see. "Me and Jake'll make a group of two." He pointed at the map spread across the coffee table. "Post up here, either side of this one. They're what, six a piece?"

"One of 'em has eight," Jake said. "This one here. Or, I think one of 'em got shot. So maybe seven."

"Well, is it seven or eight?" Ray demanded.

"Call it eight to be safe," someone suggested. "So... deer rifles. We get a good view, line 'em up, take 'em out fast. *Boom, boom, boom.* Hit 'em before they know what's up. Get the one with the radio first."

"Comms guy was in the middle, pretty sure," Jake offered.

"Then we focus on that guy first. He goes down, we pick off the others. This patrol here, see... you put a rifle here, here, and here. Wait 'til they git in the kill box, here. Then they got no cover, no idear where the shots comin' from."

"Yeah, okay." Ray nodded as the plan gained footing in his mind. "I see that. Easy. And once we got their gear, we hit the compound." He turned. "You know where it is?"

"Heck, no." Lerlaine placed the voice as Jake's although she couldn't see him. "I ain't got that close, but it's gotta be in here somewhere. Patrols are all about the same distance out. Like a box, see?"

Ray nodded. "We get up there, can't miss it. We get their radios, switch channels, check in, then all approach from different angles."

Jake agreed. "They'll be on alert, but this place'll have one, maybe two ways in and out. Cover those, put a bullet in anyone that comes out, and we're golden."

"What about everyone inside?" someone asked. "Four patrols of six or eight? That's, what... about thirty guys? Ain't no way they've got every gun out on patrol at the same time. They've got to have double that, at least. Call it sixty, minimum. Ray, that's pretty big numbers."

Ray shook his head. "Except we know these hills. Even if these douchebags are army or whatever, what do they know 'bout hunting this terrain? We grew up here; they were in a desert for twenty years."

He grabbed his beer. "And don't forget, that place was abandoned until a few weeks ago. They haven't had time to learn. We can do this. We *have* to do this, you hear me? If we don't, these SOBs are gonna dig in and we're never gonna see the end of 'em. Then, they're gonna be up our you-know-whats. We hit 'em now, hit 'em hard, and this whole place is ours."

"Still." Ryder scratched a spot on his scruffy chin. "Even if we come at it from different angles, we'll be pretty thinned out. We need a distraction. Maybe rig up some pipe bombs?"

"You'll just set the mountain on fire, moron," someone sniped. "Another of those windstorms picks up and the whole place'll light up again."

The room fell quiet. Lerlaine nibbled on a jagged

nail. Maybe she wasn't the only one who thought this whole plan was crazy.

"Ain't there a pretty big bunch of folks hunkered down at the chemical plant off 194?" Ray asked. "You was out there a few days ago, Gun, wasn't you?"

"I guess about twenty, twenty-five, maybe." Gun's voice was rough and deep from years of smoking. "Last I saw, they was still there. Didn't look like the fighting types, though."

"That don't matter. Say we give 'em a head start, tell 'em how to get up there. We hit the patrols. They move through."

Ray pointed at the map. "We hang back here, see? Kick this hornet's nest, they swarm out. All those folks from the plant will scatter and keep the hornets busy. We pick 'em off, cut down the numbers inside."

Lerlaine's gut twisted. It was one thing to shoot a bunch of military types who've been killing ordinary people left and right. But to sacrifice people just trying to get by... If they were anything like she was only a few days ago, they were half-starved, unarmed, and nearly helpless.

She wasn't the only one uncomfortable with the idea. "I don't know, Ray." Jake kept his voice even. "You sure we wanna... I mean, they'll be gunned down. No question."

"They try and cross, they'll be gunned down anyway," Ray pointed out. "They go south, they run into that Jesus-freak cult down there. They stay here, they starve. They're screwed no matter what they do. At least this way, we end up on top. We'll give 'em some pistols, maybe they'll take a few out for us. Hell, maybe they survive. Just tell 'em, see what they say."

"Alright." Gun grumbled out a response. "I'll talk to 'em."

"Tell 'em we'll keep 'em safe," Ray urged.

If Gun responded, Lerlaine didn't hear it.

With the plan settled, the conversation devolved into Ray slinging words of encouragement, boasting about how many men they were going to kill, and what kind of guns they'd find. How after it was all over, they'd have a castle they could rule from. It was laughable, even juvenile.

It was a suicide mission.

Lerlaine shivered from nerves and something else... Optimism, maybe? Ray might go up the mountain with his boys and never come back. He'd be shot and she'd be free of him forever.

There was enough food here to last, what, a few months, if she was careful with it? If she ate enough to keep Hunter fed and made sure Maddox ate just enough to stay healthy, she could stretch it to six, maybe.

Then again, if those men up in the mountain really were actual, trained military types, would they come looking to eliminate any lingering threats? If they took Ray out and figured out where he'd come from, this place would probably be swept or... whatever it was they called it.

Would she be safe?

She watched as Maddox dug around his bowl for the

last fistful of cereal. *No.* She wasn't safe here. She wouldn't *be* safe. On her own, she'd just end up where she was before—desperate and willing to make a deal with the devil to save her kids.

With Ray, it was only a matter of time before he realized that food was scarce, and maybe did something horrific. Maybe the military up on the mountain, if that's who they were, would come down, find her, save her and her children. Or maybe they would shoot first and never ask a question.

None of the options as to how this whole plan would play out were good. On the dresser across the room, the keys to Ray's race car practically called to her. He'd be gone. She could pack up, take as much food as she could, and leave.

A scrape of chairs and a thunder of boots sounded from the living room and Ray appeared in the doorway, blotting out the light. He stood there a moment, looking at her, and then at Maddox, before ducking into the closet where no door now stood thanks to too many punched holes. He pulled out his hunting jacket.

"Me and the boys are leavin'." He shrugged into it. "Gonna be gone for a few days. Don't eat all the food."

Lerlaine's voice caught in her throat like it always did when she spoke to Ray. If she said nothing, she was cold and ungrateful. If she said something, it had to be the exact right thing.

In the second of hesitation, his eyes cut toward her. "Did you hear me?"

"I did," she answered softly. "I won't eat the food. We'll be careful. W—where are you going?"

"Out," he said flatly, his eyes narrowing. "The f— do you need to know for? You think because I let you live here and eat my food and ride my junk you get to run me?"

She resisted the urge to cover Maddox's ears. She'd done that before, and Ray had almost hit Maddox in his effort to hit *her*. "You're right," she covered quickly. "I don't need to know. Just... worried about you, is all. I'll... I'll miss you. Come back safe."

He eyed her for a long, dangerous moment, weighing something. Probably deciding whether she meant it, or was placating him, or trying to 'handle' him. All things that could set him off.

Someone called from the living room. "You comin', Ray?"

Thank goodness. Ray raked fingers through his greasy hair, his eyes leaving her finally. "Hold your horses, Ryder," he barked.

Maddox flinched and watched Ray like a startled rabbit. Hunter stirred, gave the first cough of what was going to be a wailing fit soon. Lerlaine bit the inside of her lip, kept her face neutral.

Ray rolled his eyes at Hunter. "That thing never shuts up," he muttered as he strode forward. He leaned over the bed and grabbed a fistful of Lerlaine's hair.

She swallowed a whimper and forced herself not to wince as she moved with his hand and let him press his lips to hers. His tongue invaded, spreading the taste of beer and the sickening, slimy bitterness of his dip over her tongue and teeth.

There was nothing sweet about it, nothing tender or loving; it was just another reminder that he kissed her like that because he could, not because he wanted to, or even wanted any kind of affection. Her heart pounded and her spine stiffened despite her best effort to let him have his way.

Animal terror filled her body as he pushed her back hard enough that she caught herself with one hand to keep from falling onto Hunter.

Maddox sniffled but choked back a cry of alarm. That was maybe the worst of it. Not that she had to suffer through it, but that her son *knew* how dangerous it was to cry out.

For half a heartbeat, she imagined Ray on the forest floor, his skull opened, his brains spread out on the ash and undergrowth, his eyes wide but blank. The thought made her hopeful, and she hated herself for it. But it would be better, that way, wouldn't it?

"Clean this place up while I'm gone," Ray muttered as he went for the door.

Lerlaine leaned into the hopeful feeling, letting it swell inside her chest. It was something to cling to in the moment. "I will," she promised, and smiled at him when he looked back at her. It was a genuine smile. She *meant* it, even if Ray wouldn't know what she was smiling at. "Good luck, baby. Stay safe out there."

Ray looked her over, momentarily confused, before

nodding as he pulled a hat from his pocket. He shook it out once and slipped over his head. "I will, baby."

The door slammed. An engine revved. He was gone.

Lerlaine gathered Maddox to her chest and squeezed him tight.

She prayed harder than she'd prayed for almost anything in her life. *Please God, let him die up there and never come back. If you have any mercy left, let him take a bullet to the head.*

She knew it was wrong to pray for his death, but she did it anyway. Over and over until her heart finally slowed and she could breathe again.

Horse Creek Base, New United States
Friday, June 18th, 1:10 pm EST

Caleb stood at ease, expression flat and businesslike.

At the comm console, Corporal Masterson had a blank, distant look on his face as he listened to the signal coming over his headphones. The radios would pass the encryption tests just fine; Caleb made sure of that. The secondary encryption scheme he programmed wouldn't kick in for six hours. If anyone else in the base had the least bit of experience with secure comms, they'd have checked the scheme, but no one present would have known what they were looking at if they'd tried.

Caleb cut a glance at General Thomas. It had been difficult to obtain access to the terminals in the security room to load encryption schemes onto the radios. But he'd not only managed it, but now had a high clearance keycard tucked in his pocket, burning like an ember that might attract attention any second.

A rough plan percolated in his head, but there were a lot of blind spots still. If he managed to make it work, he could get Elizabeth and Lana out of the base within a day.

General Thomas shifted position, watching with intense focus as Masterson flipped a switch to engage the decryption on their end, then depressed the transmission button. "Delta Team, check three. Over."

A second later, he gave Thomas the thumbs up before pulling the headphones off. "Looks good, sir. Encryption seems solid. I don't know if it would hold up against another military, but the chances anyone in the region has the equipment to crack it is slim to none."

General Thomas gave a curt nod, then looked to Caleb. "Well done, Staff Sergeant."

"Thank you, sir," Caleb replied. "I can beef up the encryption scheme to military-grade with more time. This was just enough to get us operating."

"You do that. For now, though, this will be enough to give us better security in the field. This will save a lot of lives, Machert."

Caleb knew that the lives he meant were the lives of his men, and maybe anyone willing to bend the knee. No one else counted to the general. "Yes, sir."

General Thomas studied him for a moment longer before flashing a tight smile and tipping his head toward the door. "Walk with me, Staff Sergeant."

Nothing about the general's tone gave him reason to

be nervous, but a tremor of worry ran through Caleb all the same. He waited for the man to pass and exit into the hallway, then fell into line beside him, consciously forcing his breathing to stay even to keep from showing his nerves.

They walked for some time before Thomas spoke, taking two turns to move into the officer's quarters, not far from where Elizabeth would have heard General Thomas speaking with the lieutenant two days ago.

When he did finally speak, it was with a conversational tone that Caleb seemed a little too calculated for his comfort. "We're keeping an eye on a group of apparent civilians that moved out of a chemical factory near Lansing. You know it?"

Caleb shook his head. "I'm not all that familiar with this part of the state, sir. I know where Lansing is, though. It's not far."

"Not far," Thomas agreed. "They're coming across some rough terrain. Normally it's a day's walk at most, but—well, with things like they are, that's three days at least for anyone not well supplied and disciplined."

Normally, Caleb wasn't privy to this kind of intelligence. That Thomas was telling him now seemed like another sign that something was wrong. Or had he finally gained the general's trust by securing their field comms? He couldn't read the man well enough to know.

"I take it they aren't," Caleb ventured, trying to stay neutral.

"Not as far as we can tell," Thomas confirmed. "Of

course, if they steer clear of us, there's no problem." He left the implication unsaid.

"Anything I can do, sir?" Caleb wondered. There had to be a reason for this.

"Well, I don't know, Staff Sergeant," Thomas stopped near the door to his ready room and looked Caleb in the eye. "You think there might be?"

It was a test, then. Was he willing to execute civilians if they crossed some imaginary line they didn't even know existed? There was only one possible answer. "I'd be happy to get some fresh air, General."

Thomas gave a short chuckle. "I don't know if we can call it fresh anymore. But you've got more combat experience than most of the men here, with only a few exceptions. I know it's not your typical position here, but, well, I have a team that's down a man and I don't have anyone ready to replace him."

"Which team, sir?" Caleb asked. "I hadn't heard we lost anyone."

"We've lost several." Thomas shook his head slowly as he reached for the door handle. "These people don't know what we're about, Machert. But we're going to show them soon. Report to Lieutenant Warren at 1800 hours. I'll let him know you're joining his detail."

"Yes, sir." Caleb saluted.

"Warren's a loyal officer and a fine soldier. You've impressed me, Staff Sergeant. Impress him, too."

There was a veiled warning in that, Caleb knew. Warren was the lieutenant who had suggested Caleb gave him bad intel. "I will, sir," Caleb assured him.

"Good. Dismissed." The general disappeared into his ready room.

Caleb turned on his heel to leave, picking over the conversation. He resisted the urge to pull out the keycard he'd created. Would it work? Had someone noticed that a new card had been issued? Or was this something else?

At first, he'd assumed it was a test; was he willing to execute civilians on command? But there was another possibility. He'd secured their comms as far as anyone knew. Was that the limit of his utility?

If it was, and Thomas—or Warren—thought he'd outlived his usefulness, then the general might have just ordered Caleb to his own execution.

CHAPTER TEN
LANA

Horse Creek Base, New United States
Friday, June 18th, 6:27 pm EST

Lana punched the bag harder. Her breath came quick and fast, and her knuckles ached from the workout but she didn't quit.

Working janitorial drove Lana crazy. If she'd been cleaning guns or learning the radio system or even working in the kitchen with her mother, she'd have lost herself in the task and quieted her mind for a while.

School had been like that. She could focus on studying, writing a paper, or anything related to her classes for hours while the rest of the world passed on by.

Something about mopping floors and scrubbing toilets and showers and doing laundry—all of which seemed to only ever be done by the women in the base—gave her none of that relief. Her thoughts ran on a loop, following a track that she couldn't seem to alter for more than a minute at a time.

A snippet of conversation with Jessup: the day they met, their first date of late-night pizza at the dive off-campus, the first time he'd become so absorbed in a math problem, he forgot she was even there.

His death in slow motion and all her poor decisions. She fantasized different scenarios, some ridiculous and impossible. She threw a knife into the clouding ash and struck the man who'd killed Jessup in the throat. He died, and she was Jessup's hero, and he was still with her and... doing something important on the base.

Her parents, huddled in some corner, talking in hushed tones about how fragile, or young, or plain broken she was now. Her mother wishing they had a therapist she could see. Her father thinking she needed hard work, or purpose, or something nebulous to take her mind off it all.

She punched the bag again, a quick *one, two, three*, and wiped a bead of sweat before it dripped off her chin. She *knew* it wasn't her fault. Intellectually, anyway. Jessup had saved her. He'd thrown himself in the way, and paid for it, but she was alive because of him. But it didn't stop the loop of her thoughts.

Her heart pounded in her ears and her muscles burned. In the exhaustion—the moment when she barely sucked in enough oxygen—she could almost forget it all. *Almost.*

On the verge of giving up, she relaxed her stance as

the door to the gym swung open. She looked over, half expecting to see her father, but found Derek instead.

Great. Cause that's what I need right now. More complicated feelings.

Derek stood in the open door, taking in the scene. Her, breathing hard, knuckles wrapped, sweat coating her face and neck and arms, stripped down to just the tight, regulation tank top and shorts. The bag still swung slightly from her last round. He seemed surprised to see her, or at least to see her like this. "Getting a good workout in?"

Was he nervous? Lana sucked in a breath and tried not to huff her words out. "Had some free time. Thought it would help me sleep."

"Didn't see you at mess for dinner." He stopped within arm's reach. "Glad I found you here."

Lana frowned. She didn't have a watch and hadn't looked at the clock. She wasn't hungry, but mealtimes were the only opportunity to eat on base. Snacking was strictly prohibited. "Guess I lost track."

"I was worried."

The admission caught Lana off-guard, and she turned back to the bag. "You didn't need to be." She huffed out the response between attacks. *Jab, jab, hook. Jab, jab, hook. Jab, jab, hook, grasp, knee-strike, knee-strike, knee-strike.*

Derek didn't leave. She tried ignoring him, but it threw her off. She steadied the bag and glanced over at him. He was standing, watching her, his expression pensive and pinched.

Oh, no. She'd seen that look before—the one where a guy hesitates a beat before asking a loaded question. Lana rushed out a question. "Aren't you supposed to be on patrol soon?"

Derek exhaled an unsteady breath and moved away from her to finger weights stacked on the wall beside the heavy bag. "I've got some time. You doing okay here?"

"I'm... doing fine." The question unsettled her. Had her father talked to him, or maybe her mom? Asked him to check up on her? If so, she wasn't having it. She reached for the bag and stopped it from swinging. "I kinda need some time to myself."

Derek's eyes cut toward her. "You don't own the gym, you know."

Okay—now *that* was very out of character. This wasn't about her; something was eating at him. "Are *you* doing okay here?"

His eyes fell, suddenly enamored with the cracked concrete. "I'm fine I just... I wish I'd known you were coming here instead of going to the mess. When I didn't see you I... It doesn't matter. Wanna spar or something?"

Lana exhaled and mustered up a scrap of emotional reserves left in the bottom of her proverbial barrel. She rubbed her neck, easing some of the tension, then spread her hands. "Look, Derek. I'm... touched that you were worried about me, but I think you need to know that this" —she gestured, indicating him and her—"it's not... I mean, you and I aren't..."

His brow knit.

"I like you, but I'm not in a place where I can *do* that kind of thing, okay?" Her words came out in a rush.

"Cause you've got issues," he provided the unspoken part. "Right?"

She tried not to let his choice of words get under her skin, but failed. "Yeah, I've got *issues*." She crossed her arms. "I'm allowed."

Derek's cheeks colored slightly, but he gave a snort. "You're not the only one. You think all this is easy? That I *don't* have issues? It's the end of the world, Machert; we're all screwed up."

She blinked. Jessup had been the first guy Lana ever really dated. Prior to that, her closest emotional experience with men was her dad, and he didn't do emotional stuff. Not anything difficult, anyway.

Jessup, though, didn't avoid the hard conversations, he just didn't understand his own feelings. Half the time, he couldn't put words to any of it. To hear Derek hint at his own demons... It unsettled her, but Lana did want to know. He was her friend.

She tilted her head, tried to act casual. "Do you... wanna talk about it?"

Derek's lips hardened into a thin line as he avoided her stare. "Trade you?"

She barked out a quiet laugh before lowering herself down to the rubber mat and leaned back on the heels of her hands. Derek followed, his legs crossed, elbows resting on his knees, far enough away to be casual, but close enough to have a quiet conversation.

Lana watched him for a long moment, working up

the nerve to bring up Jessup's death. After a time, she figured it couldn't be much worse than some of the stuff Derek had seen. He'd been in the middle east just before the US withdrew on combat details. Maybe it would be easier to tell him what she was going through than her dad. He wasn't so close and hadn't been there.

"You know I trekked through the aftermath of the asteroid to get here?

He nodded.

"It wasn't just my parents and me. The guy who told us how to find this place—Jessup. He was... I mean, he was my boyfriend? We weren't all that serious. Or, I don't know—maybe we were and I didn't realize it."

"He died," Derek guessed.

Lana nodded. "We caught the attention of some people, and didn't want to take the chance that they'd turn violent. But down at the supply base, right before the rock hit, they attacked us. We defended ourselves, figured they were killed in the impact, or in the aftermath, and moved on."

"But?"

She smiled grimly at the floor. "They followed us up from the supply base, tracked us through the ash and then...got the drop on us. One of them jumped me and we rolled down the mountain. It was all ash and dirt and broken branches."

She swallowed a sudden lump in her throat. "Jessup was like... this nerdy math dork, you know? He wasn't a fighter, wasn't an athlete or anything like that. And I never thought he was all that brave, really. Turns out I read him wrong. He followed us down."

She almost choked as the images flashed through her mind again. The sound of Jessup calling her name rang in her ears. "He... saved me. And it cost him."

When Derek didn't respond at all, Lana struggled to find something else to say. Some confession of guilt, but the words died in her throat, where an aching tightness threatened to choke her.

It was a long minute before either of them spoke. "You couldn't have saved him," Derek said finally. "I imagine that you probably play it through your head again and again, imagining what you could have done differently. Telling yourself a different story."

He had no idea.

"But when those things happen..." Derek shook his head, "Everything that goes down, every move, decision, reaction—it's all kind of pre-determined. Not because there's some... fate or destiny or anything like that, but because when you get right down to it, we're all just animals. We can train ourselves to do some cool tricks, but in combat, the adrenaline drives us. We act on instinct."

Lana wanted it to be true. Desperately wanted it.

Derek glanced up at her, waited until she made eye contact. "Sometimes those instincts aren't fast enough, or the other guy is just faster, or... I don't know. But it happens the only way it could have. You're not responsible for Jessup's death, Machert. But I know that it'll be a long time until you can believe that. And that's okay. It takes a long time; there's not a shortcut."

To hear Derek lay it all out caused Lana a strange mix of embarrassment and pain. As if her ordeal was so typical, so cliched, even, that everyone knew the answer and she was making too big a deal out of it. But more than that... It was like pulling up her shirt to show off a bleeding wound, making it burn fresh and sharp.

She cleared her throat. "My parents... I haven't talked to them about it much. I'd appreciate it if you don't... I mean, if they ask you, or something."

He gave her a sad, lopsided smirk. "I don't think they will, but your secret is safe with me."

She nodded absently before nudging his knee with the toe of her boot. "So that's my trauma. Pay up. It's a trade, right?"

Derek breathed a nervous chuckle and dipped his head. "Yeah, I guess. Mine is a little different."

"Bonus points if it's worse than mine," Lana said, trying to lighten the mood and failing. She leaned forward. "Seriously, you can tell me."

"I'm actually not sure that I can?" Derek rubbed a hand across his face and glanced at the door. "So... keep it to yourself, too."

She reached up with one hand and crossed her heart with a finger. "You keep mine, I'll keep yours."

He sucked in a slow breath, held it, and then eased it out as he spoke. "I'm really, really grateful to be here. It's safe, it's fortified, we've got three squares a day and fresh water. We get to shower, right? And I met you. Which... is good. Really good. But..."

Lana tried to be as patient with Derek as he'd been with her. But something dark slithered into the room as Derek spoke, something grim and ugly. His eyes were half-closed, and his nostrils flared. Lana shifted position, suddenly tense.

"The... the general, you know," he went on, barely more than a whisper from his throat, "he's brilliant. He knows what he's doing, and how to make sure we survive and come out of this better. I believe that. Some of the things he's asked us to do to get there, though..."

A breath slipped from Lana's lips as they fell open. After her mother told her about the conversation she'd overheard, she *knew* that the general's men had killed civilians. But she never connected Derek to it. Which was naïve and ignorant.

She'd been so wrapped up in her own world... "You've had to kill people," she offered cautiously. "Civilians?"

His jaw tensed and gave a short nod. "Nation building is messy," he gritted out through clenched teeth. "I get that. We... we were all left here, all these people, with nothing. My family... didn't make it out."

He balled a hand into a fist and slammed it into his open palm. "But I'm alive and we have to build something back and I *know* that means people will die. I've seen it before. I... I want to be strong enough. I keep telling myself, you know—it has to be done. They're orders, you know?"

"I know." Lana forced her voice to stay low and gentle, but she inched forward and dug her fingers into the mat. There was more under Derek's words. Something else she could see in his eyes. A sharp, awful fear. She chose her next words carefully. "Maybe it'll change. Eventually, I mean. Right?"

He nodded. "Yeah, I guess so. There's this... well. It's classified."

"Sure," Lana said, and waved it off. "I get it. I guess I was thinking"—her mind raced, trying to put together the right words that would open him up, pry loose his resolve—"that... you know... how many could there be? Civilians, I mean, coming up the mountain."

"More than you might think." He eyed her, then grimaced and shook his head. "I don't know—I mean, it's not like you won't hear about it after the fact. There's this op the general's about to pull the trigger on. Some big group of civvies are coming through."

He swallowed with a grimace. "We're gonna clear the mountain, establish a secure border. Your dad hooked us up with secure radios, so we'll have a better comms zone. Then we can finally clean house, I guess, and then everything will be a lot easier. More peaceful, you know?"

Lana's heart leaped to her throat. *Clean house.* She hid her reaction, though, and gave a weak smile. "I mean, it'll be nice to be able to go outside without worrying about who might be there waiting. You're going, then? On the op?"

"Yeah," he confirmed, his eyes going distant. "One

big push and... I doubt I'll be able to transfer out of infantry, but hopefully it'll be a lot less eventful."

If there was more to know, she didn't think Derek was going to tell her. Instead of pressing him and tipping her hand, she waited until he was looking at her again before glancing up at the clock. "Wow." She made a show of hurrying to stand. "I didn't realize how late it was. I should get back to quarters. Mom and Dad like to do this whole, *tell-me-about-your-day* thing."

Derek stood with her. "Must be nice. Thanks for talking."

Lana forced another smile. "It was good."

She knew what came next. It wasn't hard to tell it was coming, given the way Derek stiffened, his eyes drifting briefly to her lips. He rubbed the side of his neck, and then moved in, closing the space between them in one step. Lana braced herself.

Derek's lips pressed to hers—not overly aggressive, a little awkward. Still, even as her heart pounded from far more important things than a kiss, it wasn't all that bad. Derek's lips were soft, full. He smelled of salt and musk, and his end-of-the-day stubble scratched briefly at her lips.

A pang of guilt hit Lana in the gut, but she managed not to jerk away. Jessup was dead. He wasn't coming back, no matter how many times she imagined he did.

Derek pulled back with a worried look. "Sorry. I mean—not sorry, just... I should have asked, probably."

Lana cleared her throat. "You get a pass, this time.

But I really do need to go. My parents worry, you know, and we don't get a lot of time, so..."

He gave a quick, exaggerated nod and stepped out of her way. "Sure, yeah. Don't let me keep you. Uh... see you tomorrow morning?"

"Six sharp," she agreed.

She hustled to the door before glancing back. He hadn't moved. "Night, Derek."

"Night, Machert."

Lana slipped out as if she were in no hurry at all. But as soon as the door closed, she picked up the pace, barely shy of an all-out run. She didn't have time to process the kiss or think about Jessup for once. Hopefully, at least her mother was already back.

Outside of Lansing, NC
Friday, June 18th, 6:35 pm EST

Ray spat his wad of dip on the ground and flicked a clump of decaying leaves over it. Two days picking over the mountain toward the compound had sobered his mind and tightened his nerves. His temper balanced precariously on the edge of losing it and going on a rager. *This damn well better work.*

Jake crept forward in the dark a half a dozen steps ahead. Thanks to the grim reality of life in an empty town with nothing to lose, Gus hadn't needed to offer much to convince the people holed up at that chemical plant to come along for the ride.

At this point, they didn't have a choice. It was either raid the mountain compound, or die of starvation. They were back there, somewhere, and headed their way no matter what.

Too late to back out now. Not that he'd ever let on to the boys he had some doubts. Ray hitched up his pants and crouched beside Jake who'd stopped beside a gnarled hardwood atop a rise on the mountainside. Right on target. This whole operation was no different than hunting. Pick a spot, flush out the prey, keep eyes and ears open, take aim, pull the trigger.

Killing a man had to be about the same as killing a deer and these SOBs had it coming. This was *their* mountain, their home. Not some army base where guys like Ray weren't welcome. They would take it back and he'd be king. Maybe he'd even let that skank and her kids come live with him up on the hill. If she stayed in line, that was.

Jake fingered a small radio, turning the knobs and listening for activity. Each man had one, with a set of earbuds for staying quiet. Just about everyone in the hills had a pair of walkie-talkies for hunting with cell service being so spotty. It had been easy to find enough.

With any luck, they'd pick up a radio communication from the patrols and know the best time to strike. Worst case, they used them to alert the group from the chemical plant the coast was clear, so to speak. If the bastards in the base assumed the plant group was responsible for taking out the patrols, Ray and his crew could close in.

Thinking through the plan puffed his confidence and soothed his nerves. The patrol group he'd dubbed one, usually six men, all armed, should pass nearby at some point.

They could handle six, him and Jake. They just had to get the first shots off, make them count, and get the pretty boys scattering and panicked. He didn't have some delusion that it would be *easy*, exactly. But from their vantage point, they were higher than the patrol and could keep cover.

Ray clapped his friend on the shoulder. "You good?"

"Good," Jake confirmed. "You nervous?"

"Nah," Ray lied. It was early evening, not that you could tell anymore, with just enough light to aim by, but not so much that they'd be easily spotted. He knelt, scooped up a handful of the loose ash on the ground and rubbed it on Jake's coat.

Jake returned the favor, and within minutes, they were both covered head to toe in gray, like most everything else. Ray knocked fists with Jake, and they split up, each tracking the rise to a concealed point out of range of each other's rifles. Ray knelt on the ground and steadied himself against a tree and a rocky outcrop. He scanned the trees for Jake, but couldn't see him. *Good.*

After a few minutes, he settled into a pattern: scan the trees, twist the radio dial, listen for any chatter. Rinse, repeat. After an hour, something hissed. He twisted the dial back, his ears sharpened, and closed his eyes. It was static, mostly, but there was something in it. Words he could barely make out.

"Charlie... final... all quiet... over."

Jake hadn't been able to identify each patrol team,

but the radio didn't have all that much range. They were situated at the furthest point of this team's route from the base, if Jake had tracked them accurately.

It took another few moments before Ray heard the first footfalls off to the south of their position. He inhaled slowly, careful not to huff in ash through the bandana over his lips and nose. His fingers flexed on the stock of his rifle as he shifted it into a better position, pointed toward the kill box. His heart beat faster.

He found himself suddenly thinking about Lerlaine.

Maybe things would be different with her after this. He wouldn't be so stressed all the time. Wouldn't be so easy to rattle. She'd see that he could manage everything and maybe stop nagging at him all the time. Be grateful for once.

The soldiers came into view a few yards south of the kill zone. They were alert, their weapons up, barrels swinging as they surveyed the area. Ray tensed, but none of them settled on him.

He spotted one near the middle of the group—there were seven, not six, but that hardly mattered—with a bigger pack on his back than the others. A short, black antenna stuck out of one corner. That was the radio, then. Jake's target.

Ray lowered his head, peered through his scope, and angled his rifle toward one of the men up front. He followed him, and only lost sight briefly as he crossed one of the two trees between them.

The soldier came back into view. A second later, behind the patrol, something hard struck a tree. Jake had pitched a rock into the woods. The whole patrol went on high alert, guns coming up, lining up scopes with eyes. They were stationary for just long enough.

One, two, three, Ray counted to himself before he exhaled slowly and squeezed the rifle's trigger.

The two shots were so close together that they almost sounded like one. The rifle's stock bucked against his shoulder. The lead soldier's neck exploded at the same time as the one with the radio flopped backward.

Instantly, the other five scattered. Some laid cover fire, just like Ray had figured they would. A bullet struck the tree he was laid up by, spraying him with a hail of splinters that he flinched from but otherwise ignored as he tracked one of the soldiers who'd taken cover from Jake's fire.

It was a shorter affair than he expected. No drawn-out fire fight. Just five soldiers scrambling for cover. Then four. Then three. Then two.

Then it was quiet again.

Ray's pulse hammered in his neck, throbbing through his entire body. His hands shook on the rifle, and he laid still for a while, listening. Finally, he crawled out of cover. His eyes were wide, unblinking as he picked his way toward the strewn bodies. Jake emerged a second later, his rifle up and twitching from side to side.

In the distance, other shots rang out, muffled by a quarter mile or so of broken forest and drifts of ash that gathered in every concave surface. Some of it was automatic. Some had the sharp, brutally short crack of rifle fire. "They're gonna hear that at the base," Jake whispered.

Ray snorted as he knelt by one of the fallen soldiers and pried the automatic rifle from his grip. The strap was ruined, but that wasn't a big deal. He hefted it and grinned. "Won't hardly matter. He nodded toward the radio pack. "See what you can hear on that thing."

Jake trotted toward the radio as Ray moved to collect more guns. Army issue, from the looks of them. Each soldier had at least one extra magazine, some had two. He stuffed them into his jacket pockets, replaced the magazines on two of the guns, and slung one rifle across his back, another under his shoulder. He prepped two more for Jake, then moved to where Jake knelt by the radio.

"Anything?"

Jake pulled the headphones down from his ear before he waved at the radio pack where he'd exposed a number pad covered in plastic. "It's some kinda secure line. I don't know the code. I only get about every other word; I think it's broke or something. Someone got word back to the base, though, I can tell that much. They're scrambling, we gotta move in quick."

Ray spat out a curse. If they didn't entirely have surprise on their side anymore, at least they knew it. He tossed Jake a rifle, then handed him three extra magazines when he stood. "Let's move in, then."

"I can't tell if the boys hit their targets. You sure?"

Ray looked over his rifle, smiling. "No turning back now, brother. Radio the folks down the mountain that it's time to cross. Then let's raise some hell."

CHAPTER TWELVE
ELIZABETH

Horse Creek Base, New United States
Friday, June 18th, 7:03 pm EST

Elizabeth laid on the cot, fingers pressed to her forehead. A persistent headache pounded just behind her eyes. How long had it gone on? Hours? Days? She didn't have a clue.

She reached beneath her pillow and found the hard shape of a keycard there. For the moment, she left it there. If she was caught with it, there was no telling what would happen. Of course, if she didn't have it on her if she needed it...

Caleb had come to find her in the kitchen just before dinner. He'd eased up behind her as she peeled potatoes and slid his arms around her waist. At first, she'd been pleasantly surprised. But when he whispered in her ear, it wasn't anything romantic or sweet.

"Don't react," he'd whispered. "Thomas is putting me on detail with the lieutenant you overheard. I'm headed out at 1600. Laugh a little, try to make it convincing."

Elizabeth had glanced at Marta, who was obviously watching, despite her busy hands, and forced a strained little laugh.

Caleb growled softly and nibbled at her ear before going on, his hands trailing over her stomach. "There's a key card under the pillow in our quarters. Top security, it'll open any door in the base. At 2100 hours, get Lana, and leave out the back exit. I'll make sure it's clear. Tell me you'll wear something sexy if you remember how to get there."

The words had made her blood turn to ice as she scanned her memory. The back exit... Elizabeth knew where it was. She'd passed it a few times. "I'll... wear something sexy," she said, her voice shaking uncontrollably as she forced herself not to look at Marta.

Caleb kissed her neck, then withdrew a bit, made her turn to face him, and pressed his lips to hers. It was a real kiss—deep, firm, full of passion and maybe even desperation. It certainly was for her. She tried to say everything with that kiss that she couldn't have said out loud. *I'm terrified, but I trust you. Be safe. Please, God, be safe.*

When he pulled away from her, his eyes were hard and fierce. "Looking forward to it, beautiful," he said, loud enough for Marta to overhear. "See you then."

They shared another, shorter kiss before Caleb left her.

Marta looked over at her when he was gone, one

eyebrow up. "End of the world and all they can think about is you-know-what?"

She'd smiled, shrugged, and went back to her work, barely managing to peel without slicing her fingers.

Now, as she laid in their quarters on the verge of hyperventilating, a maelstrom swirled in her skull. How would they get to the exit without being stopped by someone? Even if they could justify being in that part of the base, there would be guards on the inside. What was near the back entrance? Anything she could claim she needed?

She didn't know the answers, couldn't slow her mind down enough to think rationally, and plan. If Caleb hadn't formulated the details, was it because he didn't know what she should do, either, or because he trusted her to come up with them?

If so, his trust was badly misplaced.

I'm useless for this. I'm dead weight, just like the general said about those people.

The thought wormed its way into her, and she couldn't shake it. She closed her eyes against a sudden burn. How was she supposed to do this?

The door opened suddenly, hard enough that she felt the wind of it. Her eyes snapped open, and she jerked upright, a cascade of apologies already on her lips. "I'm sorry, I was just—Lana?"

Her daughter looked out into the hallway quickly, then closed the door and hurried to the side of the cot. "Where's Dad?" Lana demanded.

Elizabeth blinked several times, confused at the

urgency. Did Lana know? "I... don't know. Outside. He... what's wrong?"

Lana's nostrils flared as she chewed her lip, then backed up and dropped to the edge of her own cot. "There's an operation happening. Derek told me about it. I'm not sure what's going on, but he seemed to think it's the next 'step' in Thomas's plan. Securing the mountain, or something. He said something about a civilian group headed toward us."

Elizabeth's gut sank. Was that where Caleb had gone? To take part in some kind of massacre? "Oh... *God.*"

"What?" Lana asked. She leaned forward, peering at Elizabeth to catch her gaze. "Mom, what? Where's Dad? Does he know about this? Does he have a plan? We can't just let these people die."

This didn't make it any easier for Elizabeth to think. She swung her legs off the cot, breathing hard. "I don't know, I... maybe."

"Okay, well," Lana pressed, "what *is* it? Mom? Jesus —Mom, *breathe.*"

Then Lana was in front of her, pulling her hands from her thighs where Elizabeth had begun to wring the fabric of her fatigue pants. Her daughter's hands were rougher than Elizabeth remembered.

"Look at me." Lana squeezed, putting pressure on Elizabeth's palms. "Breathe in. Deep. Good—hold it. Hold it. Breathe out slow, force it through your lips, like this."

Elizabeth followed along as Lana pressed her lips

together and blew a tight, loud stream of air through the small opening she made there. They breathed like that a few times, their eyes locked, until finally, Elizabeth began to calm. Not so much that she was at ease, but enough that her heart slowed, and her lungs no longer pumped so hard.

"What do you know?" Lana asked finally, still crouched in front of her. "Where's Dad?"

Hiding the truth from Lana was out of the question, of course. Still, Elizabeth had an instinct to deflect, to tell her not to worry. To keep her sheltered. *But she's not, anymore. There's nowhere to hide from this.*

She stared at her daughter. The woman in front of her, dressed in army green, a bit of grime on her face from where she must have been sweating, her hair a tangle of matted dark locks... Lana had told Caleb that she wasn't a little girl. Not some innocent college student. And she'd been right.

For a second, Elizabeth had the strange sense that, at least in the moment, Lana was more a mother or older sister than a daughter to her. Someone strong, her feet firmly planted on a foundation Elizabeth didn't see.

The feeling faded, but it left Elizabeth reeling all the same. There was no way to protect Lana. Caleb had trusted Elizabeth and she had to trust her daughter. Maybe it was true that Elizabeth couldn't do this—not on her own. But with Lana, maybe that changed. Maybe Lana was more competent, more ready, than she'd been able to see.

"Your father went out on deployment." Her voice

was rough but even. "With this lieutenant that thought he was sabotaging them. He didn't tell me why, there wasn't time. But if Derek told you about this... *plan*, then that must be some part of it. What else did Derek say?"

Lana squeezed her eyes shut, cursing softly. "He said that after the mountain was secured, they could 'clean house'. It's got to mean getting rid of people the general doesn't trust. It sounds like that could mean Dad, and that probably means us, too. Why did they think Dad was sabotaging them? Which lieutenant was it?"

Elizabeth spread her hands. "I don't know," she admitted. "He didn't give me a name. Who is Derek deployed with, do you know?"

"Warren," Lana murmured as she began to pace. "Okay, so—Dad told you something, right? What else did he say?"

Elizabeth turned and retrieved the keycard from the pillow. She held it up for Lana to see. "He gave me this. It's high security. He says it will get us out the back exit, and that we should meet him there at 2100 hours. He says he'll make sure it's clear."

Lana looked at the clock on the table between the cots. "Almost three hours from now... okay."

As Elizabeth watched, wheels turned in Lana's head. She began to pace, cracking her knuckles. "Back exit... there's a wastewater disposal site outside there. I'm not due to empty the barrels for another day, but I could say I need to do it early."

"Do you think whoever is there would go for it?" Elizabeth asked.

Lana shrugged. "Depends on who's there at 2100. It's off-shift, but I could say I'm bored, and want to get ahead. Of course, if it's someone who *knows* about this house-cleaning phase, they might have orders not to let anyone leave. If that were the case..."

Her daughter almost missed a step, and her face paled slightly as she looked away from Elizabeth.

"What's wrong?"

For several seconds, Lana stared at the door, her eyes twitching back and forth before she swallowed loudly and shivered. She straightened slightly and leveled a hard gaze at Elizabeth. "There's usually only one guard at the back entrance. On the inside, anyway. If whoever it is won't let us out, I... I can probably get close."

Get close and try to take them out, Elizabeth knew. Her breath came fast and hot. "Absolutely not," she started, "Lana, you are not going to—"

But Lana cut her off. "It's a last resort. But I've been learning fast from Derek. Close quarter stuff, grappling, throwing, locks. And anyway, getting close won't be hard. You must have noticed no one gives the women around here a second glance. We're basically invisible."

"Only metaphorically," Elizabeth argued. "Not *literally*. I don't want you *fighting* a trained soldier, Lana. That's... it's too much, you could be hurt."

Lana's expression soured to petulance in an instant. "I'm better than you think I am, Mom. I take Derek down more than half the time."

"Derek is barely older than you," Elizabeth said, even if she knew it probably had nothing to do with it. Lana had been training hard, she knew that. But this—actual, deadly, potentially *armed* combat—was very different.

"Can you just trust me?" Lana demanded. She threw her hands up. "For once, can you just... believe that I'm stronger and *better* than you think I am?"

The words cut Elizabeth deep. For a moment, she was back in their old house, hearing Lana scream at her the day she left for college. Now, here they were. And Elizabeth had already seen it in her daughter—this newfound strength. Or, maybe, she finally saw the strength that had always been there.

It didn't matter which direction they went, or how they got where they needed to go. It would be dangerous. There wasn't a *safe* path for them. And Caleb was counting on her—on both of them—to get to where they needed to be.

"Okay," she finally relented. "We have a little less than three hours. How do we play this?"

Lana relaxed some and held out a hand for the keycard. Elizabeth handed it over, and her daughter turned it thoughtfully in her fingers. "What level of clearance is this?"

Elizabeth shook her head. "I don't know. High, though, your father said."

Lana nodded and tucked it into her pocket. "Okay. Meet me in janitorial supply in... about an hour. Make a mess of the sheets; spill something, throw up on them, whatever you need to do. Then strip the bed and take them with you so no one will question it."

"An hour?" Elizabeth asked, suddenly alarmed at the

idea of being separated. "What are you going to do until then?"

Lana went to the door. "I'm going to do my job." She snorted as she pulled the door open. "And I'm pretty sure no one will even notice."

CHAPTER THIRTEEN
CALEB

Horse Creek Base, New United States
    Friday, June 18th, 7:32 pm EST

Caleb stared up at the clouded sky. No rain. No ash. Clouds hung thick and low, obscuring the evening sun. Darkness coated the mountainside.

He breathed in the putrid stank of stale breath left-over from whomever previously used the respirator he'd been issued and exhaled in a rush. The filter needed changing. He sucked in another ragged breath, distracted by the lack of adequate air.

Any kind of tactical operation would be near point-less without night gear, yet here they were. Cold bit his cheeks and ears as distant thunder rumbled somewhere down the mountain. It would storm again soon. Another ominous sign.

He stood off to the side, waiting as Warren and a

corporal he didn't know checked the last bodies of the Beta unit patrol detail.

"Three rifles missing," Warren called out. "Anyone see them?"

"Nothing here." Derek scouted an area twenty yards south.

Another junior enlisted called from the north side. "Might have been some sort of a scuffle over here, can't be sure. No weapons."

Caleb confirmed the same. "Nothing in this area." *Except dead bodies.*

Seven men, all dead. Caleb clenched his jaw as he surveyed the mountain. A pair of outcroppings flanked the dead, about sixty yards apart. Beta unit had likely come in from the west, circling around toward the second half of their route.

"Ideal spot for an ambush." Warren approached Caleb with his rifle at the ready. "Wonder how they knew?"

Caleb ignored the obvious accusation. He didn't know the terrain well enough to have leaked any information and couldn't have made contact over the comms without someone in the base knowing about it. If he had to lay all that out for the general later, he would.

He fit details of the situation together in his mind until a picture formed. "With the storms, fires, and quakes, we haven't seen much wildlife. But there's no building, no foot traffic around here for a few miles. My guess is, this was executed by some locals, probably hunters, who know the mountain well enough to pick the best ambush point."

Warren snorted out a curse. "Still think all these civvies are harmless innocents?"

Caleb never said that to Warren. He also hadn't used those words with the general, even though he'd questioned the policy. But Warren knew his opinion all the same. Thomas and Warren must have talked. *Not good.*

Derek entered Caleb's peripheral vision. "The radio's missing, sir," he reported to Warren. "Do we assume comms are compromised?"

The lieutenant raised an eyebrow at Caleb. "Sergeant?"

Caleb resisted the urge to correct the man. He hadn't been an E-5 for years. "They'd need the code for the box. Unless they got the code off one of our boys, they can't operate the radio at all."

He glanced up at the darkening sky. Had six hours passed since he enabled the encryption? *Close.* The secondary encryption scheme might have triggered by now.

He hedged. "But we have no idea who these people are, what they've got at their disposal. Probably best to assume we're not entirely secure."

Warren muttered something under his breath and spat. "Alright," he called, loud enough for the unit to hear him, "radio silent for the moment, ladies. Let's keep moving. Eyes and ears open, obviously these civvies are armed. Shoot on sight."

Caleb jerked, eyes snapping to Warren's face. He was

already staring, eyebrow quirked behind the grimy mask in an unspoken challenge.

"Problem with that, Machert?"

"Shoot on sight might be a bit premature."

The lieutenant stared him down and Caleb calculated his odds. If Warren moved on him at this range, brought his rifle up, tried to take a shot, Caleb could defend himself.

"Better them than us." Warren's stance softened and Caleb let out a trapped breath. "You think they had a conversation with our boys before they put bullets in them?"

No, they probably hadn't. Caleb shook his head and kept his mouth shut, and after a moment, Warren gave the order to move out.

As he fell into line, he caught Derek watching him. Something in the kid's eyes worried him. He stared a little too long. His Adam's apple bobbed. Nerves, obviously—but why?

The kid was close with Lana, but that couldn't be it. Had he been given the order to execute Caleb? Or at least told he might have to? Or was he worried about what happened when they found this civilian group?

Caleb shook it off. *Don't break concentration. Keep on your guard.*

They proceeded to one of the first watch points intelligence surmised might afford a glimpse at the group coming through. As they walked, it hit him: they'd heard no gunshots.

The ambush had taken place before the civilian

group could have come this far. Were there others out on the mountain? Had the group sent forward a set of scouts? If so, they might be back with the main group, armed and ready. The possibility set Caleb on edge.

Twenty minutes into the walk, Private Klein, a kid barely older than Derek and built like a squat brick wall, whistled a warning. Warren held up a fist and the unit stopped. It didn't take long to spot the movement down the mountain.

At that distance, and with the gloom growing by the second, they were difficult to count, even with a scope. More than a dozen, Caleb guessed.

Warren peered through binoculars. "That's them. Take positions. Let them get a bit closer, then we open up. See how they like it."

Caleb lowered his rifle. "Sir," he kept his voice calm and even, "I don't see any weapons on them."

The lieutenant glanced in his direction. "Good, it'll go faster."

"What I mean is, these can't be the people who ambushed Beta unit. They're too far below us." Caleb pressed on. "We're down at least seven men who can't be easily replaced. Shouldn't we question the civilians, see if there's anyone the general can use? Former military, specialists, medics?"

This, at least, Warren seemed to consider for a long moment. The population at the base wasn't infinite. Some of the men on the ground had been more than infantry or recon. Most everyone on base served multiple roles.

After a few seconds, Warren spoke up again, waving the unit close so he could keep his voice low. "Alright—Keller and Ramy, you two circle around to their six. Nichols and Warton, flank at three; Barton and Mueller, nine. Machert and Prince, you're with me on approach. Box 'em in; anyone runs, you know the drill."

Each of the eight members of the unit gave silent acknowledgments, and Warren signaled them to get to it. Three pairs peeled off and headed down the mountain. Caleb and Derek followed along behind Warren.

After a few steps, the lieutenant slowed, then waved them forward. "Take point. I'll cover our six."

Caleb almost snorted. Leave it to Warren to telegraph the obvious: he didn't trust Caleb at his back. Fair, given that Caleb didn't trust Warren on his. And, for that matter, he wasn't sure he trusted Derek there, either.

It was a tense creep down the incline because of it, Caleb's heart pounding in his ears, his breath coming hard through the respirator that refused to accommodate.

He tried to calm his nerves. *Liz and Lana aren't in immediate danger. It's too early to tell how this is going to play out. Stay focused.*

They approached the civilians with caution, creeping through the forested mountainside, careful not to snap a branch or rustle a pile of ash-covered leaves. The civilians took shape as they advanced. Caleb counted at least ten adults, a few teenagers at most, and at least three young children. All sported something on their backs, but most of the packs looked flat and empty.

None appeared armed. Not with the kind of rifles

that had made the shots he'd seen in Beta unit or anything else for that matter—no pistols, knives, not even any improvised weapons.

Before he could advise Warren, the lieutenant called out to the group. "That's far enough," he shouted. "Everyone stand where you are, raise your hands over your head, and get on your knees. You are trespassing on an NUS military outpost. You are surrounded, and anyone fleeing *will* be shot. Compliance is mandatory, no exceptions or questions. Everyone down, *now*."

Caleb's jaw clenched as a series of questioning and panicked cries rose from the group. Some made to run, but others grabbed them and pulled them down. In a few seconds, all of them, including the young children, were on their knees, their hands above their heads.

"We're just trying to get across the mountains," someone, an older woman Caleb thought, called out to them. "We don't want any trouble, really. We're unarmed. We don't even have much food, we're—"

"No exceptions, no questions," Warren repeated, and nudged Caleb in the shoulder. "Get them lined up, Sergeant. Private, you too."

Caleb's spine stiffened as the cold steel of a rifle barrel nudged his back. Warren had the advantage, and he knew it. Caleb forced a breath and stepped out from cover before moving down the incline toward the bedraggled bunch.

Eyes wide with terror tracked the three of them as they approached, dirty faces streaked with a mix of ash and tears. Parents huddled close to their children, hands and arms shaking. Caleb swallowed down a wave of guilt. He was a part of this, whether he approved or not.

None of these people looked well equipped. Maybe there was a doctor among them, but none were former military, or anyone who'd been able to think far enough ahead to prepare properly for a trek across this terrain.

Still, Caleb worked with Derek to line the group up. Two rows, one of twelve and one of eleven. Twenty-three in all. Behind them, the rear pair closed in, rifles raised.

Warren stood just behind Caleb and Derek, a few paces back. "Alright," he said loudly, "if any of you have a weapon, now is your one and only chance to lay them down in front of you. Anyone makes a move, raises a gun, tries to take a shot, *everyone* will be executed without hesitation. Am I understood?"

Though there was a chorus of murmured agreement, no one moved to put anything on the ground.

The lieutenant nodded to the team behind them. "Check 'em."

Two of the privates Caleb didn't know, a knob-knuckled pair no older than twenty, stepped up to the group and began patting them down and opening packs.

As they did, Warren spoke up again. "Anyone here have a valuable skill? Doctors, engineers, anyone with US military service?"

One man's hand lifted a bit higher. "Here." He was older, at least in his sixties, faced marked with a scraggly white beard coated in grime. Deep lines etched the corners of his eyes where ash had collected. "I'm an environmental engineer. I worked for the Bureau of Land Management. Thirty years."

"WTF?" Warren asked it under his breath, not loud enough for the crowd to hear.

"Resource management," Caleb informed him without turning around. "Waste disposal and reclamation. Forest preservation. That kind of thing."

The lieutenant clucked his tongue. "Wasn't asking you, Machert."

Caleb gritted his teeth. "Maybe radio it in, sir? He could be useful. They could all be useful. Sir."

There was a long, cold silence in which Caleb listened for any evidence that Warren was about to put a bullet in the back of his head. The slightest shuffle of fabric, the shift of ash or the crunch of dry leaves beneath. Even the rattle of the rifle strap where it hooked to his weapon.

"The general's orders are clear." Warren's response came quiet and laced with venom. "I have a list of potential personnel to look out for, Sergeant. *Environmental Engineer* isn't on it."

The knot in Caleb's stomach tightened for a brief moment before a surge of adrenaline kicked in. It flooded his limbs, sharpened his senses, cleared his mind. These civilians were not going to die. Not in front of him. Not at his hands.

He glanced sideways at Private Prince. Not Derek anymore; not Lana's friend. Either a target or an ally. Sweat beaded across the private's forehead.

If Caleb was wrong, he was about to die.

"Put them do—" Warren started.

He didn't get the order out. Caleb snapped around, rifle up, and fired. Short burst, three shots. Warren wore the same flak vest as the rest of them, but at least one shot sent a spray of blood bursting from his neck as he toppled backward.

Caleb swung around, dropping to a knee. As the barrel of his rifle swept past Derek, he caught the young private doing the same, his weapon aimed away, toward the two soldiers directly behind the civilians.

A split second later, the screams of men, women, and children filled the air as the group scattered, scrambling to get away. Chaos enveloped the area.

Derek fired. Caleb tracked the two soldiers to his left and squeezed the trigger twice. One of them went down, the other managed to take cover behind the remains of a tree, broken where the wind had cracked it in half. He laid down suppression fire, almost catching one of the civilians as he ran.

Caleb cast a quick glance to the right, registering that one of the skinny privates was down. Derek moved, heading for cover. Some of the civilians were on the ground, unmoving—either shot, or paralyzed by fear.

Whatever the case, Caleb couldn't think about them. He spotted movement at the edge of the tree, and fired again. Chunks of the trunk exploded, exposing white pulp as bark and splinters sprayed outward. He pushed off his back leg and kept firing in short, erratic bursts until he managed to gain cover behind a large hardwood.

The night lit up. Blinding white flashed in the air,

accompanied a split second later by a crack of thunder so deep and loud it rumbled through his bones. His ears rang, but it didn't matter. He was focused, calm, in control.

Caleb leaned out, spotted his target. The rifle jerked against his shoulder, but he barely heard the discharge.

Bits of wood peppered his cheeks and forehead and he flinched away. The other man's rifle sent a hail of bullets up the tree and over Caleb's head as he fell back. There was no time to confirm the kill. He twisted around, leaned out from the other side of the tree to get eyes on the others.

Derek was posted behind a short, squat rock that jutted up from the ground, huddled down to a space that couldn't have been much bigger than a large moving box. The rock was pockmarked with fresh wounds. One of Warren's men had him pinned, peppering the rock with short, tight bursts as he stepped out of cover to approach.

Caleb took aim and fired. The soldier jerked violently away and struck a tree, rattled but not injured. Derek rose and fired from behind the rock with an unfocused and panicked spray of bullets. The soldier slumped, slid sideways and dropped to his side.

Caleb swept the area, counting. Two near him. Two behind where the civilians had been. One at the tree, one between him and Derek.

One was missing.

He dropped to a knee and listened. Who didn't he see? His eyes went to Derek, now crouched once more, the barrel of his rifle swinging slowly as he searched the area. Caleb steadied himself, eyes alert, straining to hear past the high-pitched ringing in his ears.

The sky flashed again. A broad, almost slow fork of blue-white spider-webbed across the sky before it lanced the earth. Light boiled inside the clouds. A peal of thunder followed. Something wet and freezing struck his brow.

Movement. A spot of darkness to his right. He swung around, brought the rifle up, almost pulled the trigger, but stopped himself in time to see the stunned, wild-eyed face of one of the civilians.

"Down!"

He only barely heard it, but the sharpness in Derek's voice told Caleb's body to move before he had time to process it. He dropped to his side, intent on firing on the next thing he saw moving. Muzzle flash lit the darkness. A figure fell to the ground over his head, and he craned to see the silhouette of a radio pack lit by another lightning strike.

Seven. That was all. Caleb pushed himself up and visually swept the area one last time before he moved to join Derek.

Derek slumped against the rock he'd taken cover behind, his rifle sagging between his knees. He stared at the ground, panting hard, blinking rapidly. When Caleb knelt beside him, the kid didn't look up or even seem to notice he was there.

"Private," Caleb said, quiet but firm. "*Derek*. Look at me, son."

Derek lifted his face, but his eyes failed to stick to one

spot. "W-what... what did you do that for?" he breathed. "What did I... Lieutenant Warren... Barton and Ramy... I... what did I do?"

Caleb glanced around at the bodies. Here and there, some of the civilian group were moving. Some coming closer, others kneeling by fallen friends or maybe loved ones. Maybe even strangers they'd barely known. Not all of them had survived the crossfire, but it looked like the casualties were only a few.

"You've saved these people." Caleb placed a hand on the back of Derek's neck and gave him a gentle shake. "They were going to die, and we saved them. You made the right choice, son."

Derek shook his head and pulled away. "No—you don't understand," he rasped. "The general—we'll be executed. *Lana* will be... oh, *God*, it'll be my fault." A string of incoherent curses followed, and Caleb gritted his teeth.

Gentle and firm wasn't cutting it. Caleb grabbed the kid by a fistful of shirt and hauled him up to his feet. He'd have to do this the hard way.

"Look at me, soldier," he snapped. Caleb waited for the private's eyes to focus on his. "I've got Lana taken care of. She and her mother have a way out. I made sure of it before I left them. Had a feeling this... wasn't going to go well. But we're on a tight schedule."

As if in emphasis, the sky lit again with an immediate boom of thunder. Freezing rain splattering Caleb's face. A drop trickled into his eye. It *burned*.

He let Derek go, slapping at his eye as if he'd been

stung. He growled out a curse and pulled the hood of his jacket up. Derek did the same. They had to move.

Caleb looked around at the civilians and saw them covering their own heads with packs or raised jackets and hoods. "Hey!" he barked at the closest one. "You. Come here."

The skinny woman turned this way and that, convinced he couldn't mean her. After a moment, she stepped cautiously forward, eyes trained at the ground. "T-thank you," she stammered. "For..." A sob cut off the rest.

There was no time to soothe her. Caleb got to the point. "There could be more men coming. Get the survivors back down the mountain, out of the way."

She shook her head, meeting his gaze for the first time. "We can't travel in this."

"Why?" Derek asked.

"It's acid," she told him. "It's been pouring down out east, coming this direction. We need to get into cover."

The only cover anywhere nearby was the base. Caleb grunted and rubbed at his eye again, trying to work out what to do. He looked around the scene. The rain fell faster, splattering loudly on his hood. "Alright, look," he said, and pointed to Warren's fallen body. "Anyone who can hold a rifle, point it, and shoot it—get them a gun. The base is that direction"—he pointed up the mountain —"but it's not safe yet. There's someone else out here, they took out some of our people."

The woman nodded. "I know. Some... people—we don't know them. They found us in Bina, told us to come along behind them. They said they'd clear the way for us."

The missing piece of the picture snapped into place. "Did they, now?" he wondered. He glanced at Derek. If the private had put it together as well, it didn't show on his nearly blank expression.

They'd gotten radio chatter about the group. These people were a distraction. Whoever had killed Beta unit —and maybe others—were still elsewhere on the mountain. "Any idea how many of them there were?"

She shook her head. "We just saw two of them. They didn't tell us anything more than that."

"Military?"

Again, she shook her head, adding in a shrug. "I'm sorry, I... if they were they didn't say, and I wouldn't be able to tell by looking. We were just relieved someone was going to help us get across. More people are coming —a lot more. The coast... it's Hell."

She pulled her jacket closer. "There's no food. Tidal waves came, one after another, with the earthquakes. Everyone who survived is coming this direction. We don't even know one another very well. We just kind of... ended up together. We were afraid to come over the mountain. Some people came up, and... managed to get away."

But still, they'd tried to come now. Caleb spared a glance at his watch. 19:50. Not much more than an hour before he needed to have the back entrance to the base cleared. It would take only a little less time than that to get there. But he had to know. "Why did you come this way?" he pressed. "Why not cross further south? Or further north?"

The woman laughed bitterly. "North of here is just as bad as the coast. There's at least one with us who came down. There are still fires, there hasn't been as much rain. And south? People say there's some kind of... I don't know, a militia, or a cult, or something."

Caleb groaned to himself. So—north was out, south was out, east had already not been an option. That only left west. Well, at least he knew.

He hefted his rifle to hold it across his stomach, lowered but ready. "Arm some of your people," he told her again. "Don't follow too close. Don't engage if you don't need to. Stay low, try to stay out of sight. But defend yourself if you must. These people will shoot on sight."

She gave a shaky nod and watched him and Derek both as they withdrew.

Caleb looked at the private, assessing whether he was in any shape to help.

As if he could feel the question, Derek glanced at him. "I'm good."

"You sure?"

Derek's jaw hardened, his eyes cleared some, and he exhaled a steady breath. "I'm good for duty, Staff Sergeant."

Maybe it helped the kid to identify Caleb as his C.O. Gave him a sense of certainty. Caleb had missed that himself at times. Maybe that was why he'd been so willing to look past things that now seemed like loud warning bells since they'd been brought into the base.

That changed now, he promised himself. *Time to stop thinking there's any semblance of normal to get back to. From now on, it's just me, Lana, and Elizabeth. Everyone else is a potential threat.*

It was the only sure way.

He clapped Derek on the shoulder. "Let's get moving, Private."

Outside Lansing, NC
Friday, June 18th, 7:50 pm EST

The patter of gunfire echoed between bursts of thunder. Ray froze and listened. Jake hunched low to the ground. Semi-auto, three burst shots. Not hunting rifles.

A droplet of rain landed on Ray's hand and pain welled at the site. He pulled his hood up and jabbed Jake with an elbow. "It's raining, dummy."

Jake wouldn't look at him.

"What's the matter with you?"

Jake stared past him. "Those people. The... the guns; those were military. They... they killed 'em, you think?"

Ray shrugged. "Your point?"

They hadn't known those people, hadn't even met them—Gun and Ryder had convinced them to come up.

He gave Jake a shove to shake him out of whatever guilt thing he had going on.

"Now all those military types think they solved the problem. They'll relax for a bit. This is what was supposed to happen, remember?" He nudged him again. "They was just a bunch of idiots who wouldn't have made it over the mountains anyway. This way, they died quick. Better than starvin' and freezin' to death."

"I guess." Jake didn't look convinced.

Whatever. Jake was too sensitive. Always had been. Still, the last thing he needed was for his right-hand man to get trigger shy now. He gripped Jake's jacket near the neck and pulled him around to face him. "Look at me," he demanded.

Jake blinked against the rain pelting the lower part of his face as he looked up. "We gonna have a problem? Because we're about to kick the nest, and I can't have you all choked up about some idiots you didn't even know. Lots of people are dead, Jake. You ain't all screwed up about them, are you?"

"I..." Jake's jaw snapped shut, his eyes dropping.

Ray rolled his eyes. "Brother, you wanna mope and be all depressed and weepy; *fine.*" Ray let him go, gave him a hard enough shove that Jake had to step back to catch himself, then jabbed a finger at his friend's chest. "Do it on your own time. Right now, you better pack that business up, bury it somewhere deep enough it'll smell like crap tomorrow, and keep your eyes on the prize. Don't wimp out on me now."

Jake rubbed his chest where Ray had jabbed him and

managed a nod. When he spoke, his voice was at least a little firmer, like he'd picked his balls up off the ground and reattached them. "Yeah, Ray." He licked his lips. "I hear you. I got your back."

"Good," Ray grunted. He looked north, toward where the base had to be. "Eyes and ears, and gird your loins. Place has gotta be close by. Move."

Another peal of thunder followed them up the slope, lightning crackling in the clouds above, as the rain fell harder.

CHAPTER FIFTEEN
LANA

Horse Creek Base, New United States
Friday, June 18th, 7:55 pm EST

No one ever looks at you when you're working. Stay calm. Don't be an idiot.

Lana steeled herself as she knocked on the armory door. The key card dug into her hip where she'd taped it to her skin next to the spray bottle, but she dared not use it. Not yet. The armory was always guarded.

Please be some new guy. She crossed her fingers and waited. After a moment, the door opened halfway. An unfamiliar face stared her down, frowning and suspicious as he took in the lack of rank insignia and name tape—a sure sign of civilian staff. "What is it?"

Lana tugged her mop and bucket into view. "Janitorial." She plastered on a smile.

He wasn't amused. "There's no janitorial this late."

Lana dipped her head. "Yeah, I know. It's supposed to be 0800 hours tomorrow. You can check the schedule. Lana Machert." She flicked her eyes up and ran her teeth over her lower lip. "There's not much traffic overnight and I need some time off in the morning."

"Not my problem." The door began to close.

"Man, come on." She groaned and lowered her voice. "Look, I'm... I'm about to start my *flow*. I get cramps in the mornings, and there's barely any tampons in supply so I'm gonna be bleeding through my uniform and—"

"Gross, stop," the soldier grunted. Instead of shutting the door in her face, he paused and looked her over, considering. An altogether different expression congealed on his face as his eyes raked down her body. "You get extra horny before your period? I had a girl-friend who was like that."

No freakin' way. Lana shoved down the disgust and resisted the urge to cringe. She looked the soldier over slowly, cleared her throat, and glanced back down the hall.

"Look—I gotta do my work, and I don't have a lot of time." She bit her lip and lowered her voice. "But... I do have to come back this way after. Your shift runs until 02:00?" He could think whatever he wanted. She didn't mean a word of it.

The soldier's lips curled. "03:30." He stepped back to open the door. "Come on in, sweetheart."

Bingo. She pushed the bucket into the room with the mop handle. "It won't take me long."

If it had been one of the two guards she'd already shot down, this never would have worked. But this guy? Easy peasy. She waited as he returned to his desk by the door and smiled again as she pulled the mop free to slop bleach and water onto the floor. She'd used a *lot* more than the usual mix and the fumes stung her nose immediately.

The guard noticed right away, too, rubbing at his own nose as the smell broke the mood. He barked out a cough and picked up a book left half open on the desk.

Satisfied he was engrossed in the book and no longer watching her, Lana moved around behind him, slopping more water onto the concrete floor, intentionally loud enough to get his attention if he was being vigilant. No movement. No acknowledgment. *Good.*

The camera above the desk pointed at the door, not at the corner behind the desk. She glanced up at it once just to be sure, and didn't see the tell-tale blinking light in the dark little blister looking at her. *Now or never.*

With her eyes on the back of the soldier's head, Lana reached under her uniform top and retrieved the spray bottle full of ammonia she'd tucked into the top of her pants and taped to her stomach. The tape came away with minimal noise and she sloshed the water in the bucket again to cover it up. She twisted the top off while she hugged the mop handle.

She sucked in as deep a breath as possible and held it as she poured the ammonia into the bucket. *Five, four, three, two...* She kicked hard and the bucket fell over, bleach and ammonia sluicing across the concrete. She danced away from it and toward the guard, bumping into him.

Startled, the guard looked down at the sloppy mess and lifted his boots briefly before he cursed and shook his head. He elbowed her away from him and toward the desk and Lana seized the opportunity, grabbing the radio and shoving it into her pocket.

The soldier muttered a string of curses in her direction. "You better not have gotten bleach on my pants."

"Sorry, sorry," Lana said quickly, and set the mop aside as she hastened around the water and toward the door. "I need to grab something to clean this up. I'll be back."

He sighed and rolled his eyes before hitting the button on the wall beside the desk to buzz the door open. By the time Lana was through and back in the hall, her nostrils burned from the mixing of the fumes.

As the door shut, she tugged the key card free and turned to the keypad. With the cancel and enter buttons pushed, she swiped the card over the reader. She'd seen people locking doors this way before. At least, she was pretty sure that was what they'd been doing. A second later the pad gave a plaintive *beep-beep* and Lana sagged in relief.

The room was small and not well ventilated at this time of night when the air pumps were off. She'd mixed at least a gallon of bleach and ammonia. *It will work. It has to.*

Sixty seconds came and went. The guard pounded on the other side. His voice was muffled, undecipherable.

Was anyone watching on the camera? Listening in the hall?

She spun. No one. A series of violent strikes followed. Lana listened—not just to the door, but for any commotion in the hallway.

It was risky, this plan. If someone in the security office glanced at the monitor for this room, she was screwed. But there hadn't been another way. She needed access to the armory. She needed to protect herself and her mom. She wasn't losing her like she lost Jessup.

They couldn't escape unarmed.

The pounding stopped. Lana sucked in another deep breath and pulled her shirt up to cover her mouth and nose. She held the cancel and enter buttons again, swiped her card, and unlocked the door. The guard lay sprawled on the floor, bleach water soaking into his pants, head lolled to one side.

Unconscious? Dead? She couldn't think about that. She slipped her arms under his shoulders and braced her heels against the floor. He had to weigh close to two hundred pounds and Lana strained to move him.

The water helped, slicking the concrete enough to reduce the friction. She hauled him to the chair and grunted with effort as she dragged him up into it. His head slumped forward and banged on the desk. She winced, but he didn't even groan.

She propped his arms up, setting the scene like he'd fallen asleep on duty. It wouldn't fool anyone for long.

She tore the keys from his pocket and hurried to the lockers. She retrieved two handguns, loaded them, and snagged extra magazines for each, before wrapping it all in a trash bag. In another locker, there were a few knives. She considered them for a moment, then collected two of those as well, just in case. *Derek's lessons better pay off.*

Her eyes watered and her lungs burned. She'd been in the room too long. She coughed hard and forced the air out of her chest, refusing to take another breath as she shoved the trash bag in the bucket and covered it with the mop head.

By the time she managed to hit the button to let herself out and get into the hallway, her whole body shook from lack of oxygen. She pulled her shirt down and gasped in fresh air.

Lana took a final glance at the door to the armory. If he wasn't dead already, the guard might suffocate with all the fumes. The thought shook her, made her guts twist horribly until she almost thought she'd be sick. *It's just fumes. Don't wimp out now.*

She forced herself to walk away. She hurried down the hall, listening for the sound of boots on concrete. Nothing.

If a soldier glanced at the camera feed now, he would see a guard taking a nap and some spilled water on the floor. Worth sending someone to check it out? She didn't know. But it was already 2040 hours; twenty minutes until they were supposed to be at the back entrance.

If they were lucky, they'd be outside by then.

She reached the janitorial station and relief flooded her as she eyed her mother, waiting for her.

"What took so long?" Elizabeth rushed forward,

hands twisting in front of her. "I got here half an hour ago, I thought—"

"I had to wait for the shift to change in the armory."

Elizabeth frowned. "What... why?"

Lana knelt at the bucket and pulled the trash bag free. "Why do you think?"

Her mother stared at the bag, the color draining from her face. But she gave a slow nod. "Right. Okay. What... what now?"

"Now the next part." Lana tore the bag open and retrieved both a handgun and a knife to hand over to her mother. "I don't think you're going to like it."

Horse Creek Base, New United States
Friday, June 18th, 8:40 pm EST

Ash and grit wormed their way beneath Caleb's shirt as he belly-crawled toward the base of a tree. Thirty yards out from the south entrance of the base, the gnarled tree roots gave him cover as he checked his watch.

Derek eased up beside him and motioned toward the rear door of the mountain top facility. "Any activity?"

Caleb shook his head. Like the front, the rear door blended into the terrain, with a plain steel door sandwiched between a few feet of nondescript concrete. Two guards leaned against the concrete, faces obscured by respirators as grimy as Caleb's own.

The growing storm and the gloom were on their side. With limited sight lines, the guards might miss their approach, especially if they came at the door from the west.

"No alarms," Derek muttered.

"Just the two usual guards, as well. Half expected more."

Derek lifted his binoculars, but they weren't much use. After a moment, he put them away. "You sure? I can't see anything."

Caleb pointed to the entrance. "Move your eyes back and forth. It'll refresh the cones in your eyes, they'll pick up a bit more light, and your brain will piece it together."

For half a second, Derek gave him an incredulous look. But then he turned his attention back to the base. After another silent moment, he gave a soft snort. "Where'd you pick that up? This what they teach Marines?"

"YouTube," Caleb admitted. "Lana went through a ninja phase when she was nine."

Derek suppressed a laugh. "That tracks, I guess. You know, she's good at the close quarters stuff. Picks it up fast. She... said you and her used to practice some?"

"Yeah." Caleb didn't elaborate. Now wasn't the time to bond over his daughter, or whatever the private was trying to do. Caleb needed to focus and stow the worry for his family for the moment. And feeling anything for the man next to him was dangerous at best. No matter how they cut this, one way or another they were going to be back under fire. It was just a question of when, where, and whether they were prepared.

He checked his watch again, angling it to catch a flash of lightning that lit the clouds. "Ten minutes."

Derek sucked air through his teeth, still watching the guards. "They're coming up from below?"

"That's the plan. Lana and Liz will figure it out."

"But—" Derek hesitated.

"Spit it out."

"The guys inside have to call up a confirmation before the outside guards will open the door, and they have to confirm before they'll open up downstairs. Security protocols. If these guys don't answer, whoever's on duty inside won't open the elevator for them. If Lana doesn't have the code, the guards up here will cut the elevator and call it in."

Caleb swallowed a curse. He hadn't known the details of the procedure. That gave them, at best, a very small window between Lana and Liz getting into the elevator, somehow, and Caleb taking the guards out. At worst, his family would never make it into the elevator at all.

Blood whooshed in his ears. "Ideas?"

Derek stared off into the distance for a long moment nudging Caleb's shoulder. He pointed to one side of the base entrance.

Caleb squinted into the gloom until he caught movement. Two shapes passing between the trees, visible only in the intermittent glow of lightning in the distance. He squinted harder, trying to piece out more than a smudge. Was that a rifle?

The shapes crouched, nowhere near full height, and

moved slowly and full of deliberation. Hunters, he guessed.

"Think those are the guys that took out the patrols?" Derek whispered.

It couldn't be anyone else. Not unless some of the civilians had armed themselves and then suddenly gotten a whole lot braver with rifles in their hands. These two were headed for the entrance. Was that their plan? Take out the patrols, use the survivor group from before to cover it, then get close to the base? *Then* what?

"There have to be more than two." Caleb flicked his eyes back and forth, trusting his instincts to pick up subtle movements of shadows on shadows. He tracked the two moving into a position across from the door.

It didn't make sense. "No way two people took out all four patrols without someone radioing in. They had to have spread out, ambushed them all at the same time. Otherwise, someone would have called it in, and this place would be crawling with soldiers."

Derek leaned out to scan the mountain. "So—what, three more teams?"

"They'd split up evenly. Two here means there's as few as eight, as many as... eleven." Caleb's jaw clenched. "They want inside."

If what Derek explained was true, with the first shot, the base would lock down. A single radio call and Liz and Lana would never escape. All the people coming up the mountain would, what? Die from acid rain exposure? After everything?

"They're gonna screw this up." Caleb groaned out a

curse and tugged on Derek's shoulder. "We have to either take these guys down or get them working with us before they trap Liz and Lana inside and cut us off."

He checked his watch. *Eight minutes.* Eight minutes to keep his promise to his family. Whatever happened next, he was getting them out of there. Elizabeth and Lana would make it.

Just get to me. That's all you have to do. I'll handle the rest.

CHAPTER SEVENTEEN
GENERAL THOMAS

Horse Creek Base, New United States
Friday, June 18th, 8:40 pm EST

General Thomas stood in the situation room, knuckles pressed to the plastic folding table he'd commandeered for his personal use during the operation. So far, Warren's unit hadn't made contact.

Three hours and no contact.

A mix of worry and anger simmered in the general's gut. Anger at Warren, Machert, the whole miserable situation he found himself in with this ragtag assortment of military retirees, failures, cast outs, and reservists who'd probably only enlisted for the paycheck.

None of them *really* understood what they were doing here. Thomas was the only one who grasped the value of the opportunity in front of them. Sure, they listened to his speeches, and parroted bits of what he'd told them—what he'd promised them. But throw a little hard work their way and, what? They crumbled?

He scanned the room. Not a man within his view understood what it meant to go weeks at a time on four hours of sleep a night and still get up and *do his job* because it meant something. Something bigger and more important than all of them.

"Can someone get me an update?" he demanded.

Every pair of eyes in the room turned to him for a brief moment before darting back to their stations.

"Sir?" Corporal Masterson squeaked out the word. "We... might have a problem?"

Thomas inhaled deeply and let the breath out in a thin stream. It was good to show anger, prove to these men he was more than in charge, he was a force of nature. But they still needed to talk. To communicate. Not shut down out of fear.

He toed the line. "We *might* have a problem, Corporal? Or do we have a problem?"

Masterson tugged the left earphone of his headset back. "Sir, the patrols missed their last check-in."

"Which ones?" Thomas pressed.

"All of them," he said. "I've been asking for updates for the last five minutes over the secure channel. No response."

Thomas straightened from the table so that only his fingertips brushed the edge, splayed out in front of his hips. "No response or no message going out? Can you tell if they're receiving the transmission?"

With a grimace, Masterson turned back to his blocky

laptop and muttered to himself while the General waited impatiently for an answer. It would probably take time, and possibly be the wrong one—Masterson wasn't any kind of comms technician; he'd had to learn from manuals after Private Carson had been found speaking out of turn.

Thomas reflected, briefly, on the need to implement a cross-training program on the base. It was a bad idea to concentrate specialist skills in too few men. There was no telling when one of them would lose their sense of loyalty and focus and have to be put down. Machert was an example of that, most likely. It seemed unlikely that Masterson would be a suitable replacement for a trained comms engineer.

"Any time in the next few days, Corporal."

Masterson's body language became nearly frantic. He finally pulled his headset back entirely and turned in his chair, his face white with fear. "Uh... Sir, I... there's something off with the encryption program." He swallowed so hard Thomas heard it from three yards away. "None of the codes seem to work. I tried the non-secure channels, even. No response."

A cold fury swelled in General Thomas's chest. He had a strong urge to flip the table in front of him and grab Masterson by the lapels. But raging would make him look helpless, out of control. His fingers dug at the plastic. There was only one reason the codes didn't work.

Machert.

"Corporal, did you not thoroughly *test* the secured radios?"

"I... yes, sir," the corporal stammered. "I did, sir, I—it was a full diagnostic, all the standard tests, it was *working* before, I don't... sir, I'm *not* an engineer."

No, but Caleb Machert was. And Thomas didn't have a single doubt he was behind the sudden blackout. "Traitor," he hissed.

Masterson's eyes grew wide and white.

Thomas ignored the man's fear. The corporal could stew in it, let it make his future efforts a little more thorough. "Fix it," he growled. "Reset the whole system if you must. And get me eyes on Machert's wife and daughter. I want them in custody. *Now*."

Horse Creek Base, New United States
Friday, June 18th, 8:50 pm EST

Very few of the general's men were hardened veterans. Maybe that was why the two men that Caleb and Derek managed to sneak up behind had managed to take out at least one of the patrols. Because these, Caleb decided right away, were *not* career military.

"The heck are they?" one of them asked. "Click the radio again, Jake."

Jake grumbled something that was swallowed up by a rolling growl of thunder. When it passed, he shook his head. "No answer. Just static. You think they got hit?"

"Naw," the first man said. "If they was, we'd know. They'd have folks out here huntin' us down like pigs. Try again."

"It ain't workin', Ray," Jake hissed. "And I'm getting a

freakin' rash on my hands, this crap itches. We need better cover."

"Quit whining," Ray growled back. "It won't burn your skin off, it's just a stupid rash. Grow some balls. If we need to, we take those guards out, go in, find a spot to hole up and shoot whatever fish is in the barrel."

That was a suicidal idea. No, these men were local militia, maybe—the sort that had far more grandiose ideas about soldiering than they realized and watched too many action movies.

He gave Derek a nod.

They rose silently and crept forward toward the pair of prone men. By the time one of them—Jake—glanced back and spotted them, there was no question about who would very quickly win any kind of struggle.

"Let go of your weapons," Caleb said softly, "and crawl backward until I tell you to stop."

Jake began to crawl, leaving his rifle in front of him. Ray, on the other hand, held very still—exactly like someone about to roll over and try his luck.

Caleb jerked his chin at Derek, and the young soldier slid smoothly forward and lowered his knee down between Ray's shoulder blades and neck. Almost casually, he slipped the rifle strap free, then pressed the barrel of his own to the back of Ray's head.

"Let it go, and you'll be fine. Hang on to this, and you've got until the next crack of lightning to keep the back of your head."

There was a pause. The clouds rumbled softly, flickering with barely contained lightning. Ray let go, and

Derek withdrew with the weapon in hand. He put it down a couple of yards away, his own rifle still trained on Ray's back.

"Move," Caleb warned him.

Ray moved, pushing himself back along the ground beside Jake until Caleb was comfortable, they wouldn't be seen. He squatted down beside Jake and Derek mirrored him on the other side of Ray. "Roll over, both of you."

Jake moved first, again. Ray did so only reluctantly, and then glared up at Caleb in the gloom, his face briefly lit by another flash of lightning.

When the thunder passed, he spat as he looked Caleb and Derek over. "Guess they was lookin' for us after all, huh Jake?"

"You two took out the patrols?" Caleb wondered.

"All four."

"Strike one," Caleb told him, and looked up as the thunder rumbled again, or an echo of the last peal returned to them. "Here's how this works. You get to three and I put the two of you out of my misery. How many others are with you?"

"Nine," Jake said quickly.

Ray snarled at him. "Shut yer mouth, Jake."

"I don't wanna die, Ray," Jake shot back. He raised his palms a little, almost pleadingly, looking up at Caleb. "I really don't wanna die, mister. You folks—you was killing people. We just came up to try and help folks get over the mountains safe and sound."

"No, you didn't," Caleb said, and leaned in close, the

barrel of his rifle grazing the man's jaw. "You used those people as a distraction. Who are you? And answer quick. I don't have all night."

"I'm Jake. That's Ray. The others are Gun, Ryder—
"

"Not your *names*," Caleb interrupted. "Who *are* you? Why are you here, where'd you come from, what do you want? We heard you talking. You really think you're going to just get into the base and then, what, fight off every soldier inside?"

Ray and Jake traded looks. Ray's was defiant, still; Jake's was desperate. Another crack of lightning burst across the sky. Thunder followed and brought with it harder rain.

"Can you let us sit up?" Ray complained. "The rain's in my eyes. It burns."

Caleb gave Derek a nod, and they scuttled back a couple of paces. Taking that as the permission it was, the two other men sat up and tugged their hoods forward before rubbing their eyes.

"You two... *folks*," Ray said carefully, "don't seem like you're with the base."

"We were." Caleb glanced at Derek. His face was unreadable in the dark. "Now we're getting out. I have to collect my family, they're due to come up in about five minutes. Maybe sooner. We need it to be *quiet* for that to happen. You let me get them out, you can have the base. I don't care. But you're gonna get yourself killed if you just charge in."

"Oh yeah?" Ray wondered, looking between Caleb

and Derek. "And what were *you* two gonna do? 'Charge in' professionally or some crap?"

There wasn't time to argue. Caleb highly doubted these men could be trusted. In fact, he was certain they couldn't. But they were potentially useful if they could be used the right way. "You've got nine other people?"

"Yeah," Ray growled, shooting a furious glance at Jake. "Nine."

"Radio your people," Caleb told him. "Tell them channel 12.4."

"Radio don't work," Jake said.

Well, that was a good sign. "It does," Caleb told him. "The towers up there are just scrambling everything except that channel. Repeat it three times. The comms inside won't pick up anything on 12.4, I blacked it out before I left."

Derek peered at him, and Caleb felt the accusation in his eyes. He could deal with that later if he needed to, though. "Do it."

Jake tugged his radio up, squeezed it, and spoke into it. "It's Jake. Change to channel twelve point four. Repeat, twelve point four. That's twelve point four. Over."

Once he was done, he held the radio near his face and clicked a button on the side. A second later, someone's voice came over. "Gun," a man said. "Thought we was going black ops here."

"Tell them to circle around to the south side of the base," Caleb said. "All but one team; leave them on the north entrance. They're going to meet you about fifty yards that direction"—he pointed south, away from the base—"there's a small outcrop. Hunker down there and wait. I'll signal you when it's safe to come up."

Ray gave a snort. "You ain't been out in one of these storms yet, have you?"

Caleb hadn't, and didn't like the tone in Ray's voice. "Why?"

"Mother—*Mister*," he said, eyeing Caleb's rifle, "it'll rain for *days*. It's acid rain. A little bit's a bad rash. Traveling in it? It's a death sentence."

Caleb swallowed.

"Ain't nowhere close to get out of it," Ray continued. "Hike down the mountain back east, maybe, and if you make it past the wind and lightning, and aren't too burnt up, maybe you find a house that's got a roof that'll hold up. Maybe not."

Derek breathed out a curse.

Caleb exhaled and glanced toward the base entrance, then his watch. 20:58. He couldn't wait any longer. "So, the only place to keep out of the weather is the base." Exactly what the woman on the mountain claimed earlier, but Caleb hadn't believed it. She wasn't from around here, didn't claim to have experience with the rain. He'd assumed it would quit soon. That they could weather it with a coat and a hood. But did Lana and Elizabeth even have a hood?

He thought about Maria, but the research facility was out of the question. If Maria was even alive at this point, the air quality would be barely passable for two people. It wouldn't work. Not without new filters which were inside the base.

His thoughts raced to piece together something— anything—that resembled a reasonable strategy. He didn't have one. And he was out of time. He turned back to Ray. "Get your people to the outcrop. I'll give you the signal. Follow orders, do what I tell you. Work with me, and we *might* be able to clear the base if we're smart about it."

"F— you," Ray drawled, chortling as he shook his head. "This is my operation, you fu—"

Caleb lowered his rifle to the man's face and looked to Jake. "If I blow Ray's head off, Jake, will you take orders?"

Jake sat frozen for several seconds, then nodded.

Caleb tilted his head at Ray. "So?"

Lightning flashed. Thunder cracked. Ray's mouth was twisted into a fury. But he turned his head and spat. "Sure thing."

"Good." Caleb stood. "Get moving. There are survivors from the group you sent to get murdered in the woods further down. They'll head this way. Don't shoot them."

"Aye, Captain," Ray grumbled as he stood as well and brushed himself off.

Caleb signaled Derek to go ahead of him. He spared Jake and Ray a final glance as they made their way toward the entrance, his body tensing when he saw Ray dip to pick up his rifle. But the two men turned away from them and headed away.

"He's gonna screw us," Derek warned.

"Yeah," Caleb agreed as he knelt by a tree and raised the rifle scope up to peer through it, using the strobing lightning in the clouds above to get a clear shot as Derek lined up his. "Probably."

Caleb's watch gave a single beep. 2100 hours.

He and Derek squeezed their triggers at the same time, just as one of the guards raised a radio to his mouth.

CHAPTER NINETEEN
ELIZABETH

Horse Creek Base, New United States
Friday, June 18th, 8:50 pm EST

Elizabeth padded along behind Lana and the large blue plastic barrel Lana pushed ahead of them. She inhaled and tried to count to three. Only made it to one and a half before breathing out and sucking in another tortured breath. At this rate, she'd hyperventilate before they even made it down the hall.

Her fingers shook. Sweat slicked her brow. She gasped for air.

Lana glanced back at her. "It's just ahead." She paused, frowning. "Mom?"

All Elizabeth could do was nod erratically and wave her daughter on, hoping she got the message. If she tried to speak, it was going to come out in a wail. *We're going to die. Lana's going to die in front of me.*

"Mom," Lana whispered, as she let go of the waste-water barrel and took Elizabeth's hands. "I *need* you to be strong for me."

Elizabeth shook her head. "I... I'm sorry, I can't. I *can't*, Lana, we're going—"

Lana pulled her into a hug, wrapping her arms so tight, Elizabeth could barely breathe. She returned the embrace, smothering a wave of agonizing fear threatening to burst from her throat.

"Ten minutes," Lana said into her hair, softer than a whisper. "Can you just... just pretend, for ten minutes, that we're invincible? That we have nothing to be afraid of? Something. Anything. Ten minutes, Mom, that's all we need."

Ten minutes. Invincible for ten minutes. Can I do that? She nodded. "I'll try."

Lana kissed her cheek. "You and me, we're gonna kick some butt. No one will know what hit them. And when we tell Dad about it, he's gonna tell you that you're amazing, and—as gross as it is to think about—he's gonna want some time alone with you afterward."

At that, Elizabeth nearly laughed. "I, ah... I won't tell him you said that." Lana began to pull away, but Elizabeth held on. "I know there's no time, but... I love you, okay? More than you can possibly know. No matter what's going on, and whether you can talk to me about it, or if you think it's too much, or you feel like you..."

She stopped the ramble and managed a small smile. "Even in the moments that you're not sure you can love yourself enough, you need to know that I do. That I always will. Your father, too."

Lana blinked hard, nostrils flaring as she sucked in a breath. "Yeah, Mom. I know. I love you, too. Ready?"

She wasn't, not really—there was no being *ready* for something like this. Not when Lana thought it was dangerous enough that they needed to be armed. But she followed her anyway, to the end of the hall and then around the corner, where two guards leaned against the wall near the door to the elevator.

The entryway was a small space, only wide enough for the two of them to squeeze around the edge of the barrel. As soon as they came into view, both guards pushed off the wall and shifted their rifles into a ready position.

Elizabeth felt small and weak. No match for a pair of guards with rifles.

"Need to haul the wastewater out," Lana said easily, as if she'd done this a hundred times before. "Weather's getting bad up there, and I might not get another chance if it's gonna pour for the next three days."

The guard to the left of the door shared a look with his partner, then smirked. "Oh, yeah?" He eyed the barrel. "Looks about half full."

"The other barrel is completely full," Lana shot back. "Full of some nasty slop. Like everything you washed down the shower drain last night." She made a lewd gesture at her hip, in view of the guard on the right. "So let us dump this one and then we'll be back with the next one, so you and your buddies can tend to your needs in the shower instead of into your mom's old socks."

Elizabeth knew her daughter was trying to leverage a rapport with the men, but her cheeks heated to hear Lana talk like that. Where had she even learned it? Not from Caleb. Probably from Derek. *One more reason we absolutely must get out of this place.*

She cleared her throat. "Lana—language, please. Sorry, boys."

The guard on the left shook his head slowly. "It's alright, Missus Machert. For the record, I don't use my mom's socks. I use Gunderson's."

Gunderson must have been the guard on the right because he winced at the comment. "Screw you, Rhodes."

"Right." Rhodes raised his rifle and leveled it at Lana. "And I guess screw both of you, because the general just put an APB out on your lovely behinds."

Whatever bravery Elizabeth had mustered vanished in an instant.

Lana eyed the two men and their weapons. "O-kay... any idea why? I've been scrubbing toilets all evening."

"Doesn't matter." Gunderson sounded smug. "General says you're in custody. That's all we need to know."

Lana's hand moved to the small of her back.

Rhodes' eyes narrowed. His rifle came up and he dipped his head to eye the sights.

"No!" Elizabeth screamed the word and Rhodes twisted in her direction. She watched in horror as Lana tore the handgun free from behind her back and fired.

Rhodes stumbled back and hit the elevator door. His finger squeezed the trigger too late, sending a round skittering wide to scrape across the concrete wall as he began to fall.

Lana kicked the barrel at Gunderson. It struck him, toppled sideways, and spilled foul liquid. The smell hit Elizabeth instantly, but she only registered it as a distant sensation, something coming from far away.

Lana surged forward. Gunderson lifted his rifle. Instead of firing, he snapped the butt of it forward. Lana moved so fast and so smoothly that Elizabeth almost missed it. One moment Lana twisted and brought an arm up, almost facing Elizabeth, and in the next, Gunderson was on the ground on his back, gasping for air as Lana choked him with the strap of his own rifle.

"Lana?" The word came out of Elizabeth's mouth, she knew, but it seemed like someone else said it.

Lana took one hand away from the strap, her remaining fist clenched tight around it, and pulled a knife from her boot.

"No—" Elizabeth cried. She jerked forward to grab Lana's arm, or tackle her, or she didn't even know, she couldn't let Lana...

A high-pitched whine filled Elizabeth's ears. Her vision tunneled. She gasped for air, like before, eyes wide. *She can't... She can't...*

Lana jerked her knife to one side, and the guard shuddered and began to choke. As she stood her arm, neck, face—almost the entire left side of her body—were coated in arterial blood. *Oh, no.*

Elizabeth stood motionless. Frozen in panic and fear and horror over what her daughter did. What she had to do.

Lana stood over the guard, watching him die as he gasped, thick wet breaths and exhaled muddy coughs. It only lasted a few seconds, his hand clawing at his ruined throat as if he could stem the bleeding.

Lana stared at him, eyes wide. Tears ran down her face, pale but for the dead man's blood. Her nostrils flared and her lower lip quivered.

"Lana," Elizabeth breathed. Her daughter didn't respond. Behind them, the rapid cadence of boots on concrete echoed up the hallway. The noise jump-started Elizabeth's brain. Her vision cleared. The ringing receded.

They were going to be caught.

She needed to protect her daughter. Elizabeth grabbed Lana by the arm and tugged. *"Lana."*

Her daughter snapped toward her. Her eyes cleared. Whatever was there, it fled her daughter's eyes as if she physically pushed it down.

"I'm okay." Lana lifted her free hand to her face to wipe blood from her eyes before yanking the keycard from her pocket. "What's the time?"

Elizabeth looked at her watch. "21:01." They were late. "Go, go."

Lana rushed to the elevator and swiped the card over the keypad. "Come on, come on..."

One of the radios on the guards hissed. A voice came over it. "Whiskey, Golf, Tang—"

There was a burst of static, and then quiet.

Lana stared at the silent radio. "Was that..." She swallowed hard. "Was that some kind of security code?" She cursed. "We're so close, just—"

"Lana? Liz?"

Elizabeth felt the world drop out from under her, and then catch her safely again. Her stomach swarmed with butterflies so hard that she barked a laugh and grabbed the radio. "Caleb? Caleb! We're here—the elevator won't open, we're stuck."

"Try now," he radioed back.

Lana did, quickly, and the doors slid open with a soft groan of old metal. The inner door opened next, revealing the empty inside of the freight elevator.

"We're in," Lana shouted, and reached for Elizabeth.

Elizabeth took her hand, still clutching the radio. The doors closed just as the first of the general's men rounded the corner. The elevator lurched upward. She pressed the radio to her lips. "We're... we're on the way. We're coming up."

She took a shuddering breath and sagged into Lana's arms. They were all right. They were going to be all right.

She began to smile when the elevator suddenly seized, shaking violently to a stop. Lana and Elizabeth fell back against the wall as the light went out, plunging them into darkness.

Horse Creek Base, New United States
Friday, June 18th, 9:00 pm EST

The guards fell, one like a stone, one in a slow-motion slide. Caleb dashed from his cover and sprinted to the door of the base. One of the two men was still alive when Caleb closed the distance and reached for his sidearm—intent to slow down the inevitable. Derek slammed the butt of his rifle on the soldier's temple. If the blow didn't kill him, he would be unconscious as he bled out.

Fighting cold panic, Caleb grabbed the radio from the ground near the door as he told Derek to find a key card.

"Lana?" he called over the radio. "Liz?"

There was an awful silence in response that seemed to stretch out infinitely as he closed his eyes tight and willed one of them to answer.

"Caleb?" Liz's voice came from the radio, loosening

the painful knot that had wound around his heart. "Caleb! We're here—the elevator won't open, we're stuck."

He snapped at Derek, waving his hand until the private pulled something from the unconscious guard's pocket and pressed it into his palm. Flat, plastic. The key card. He stood and swiped it over the pad too quickly, then again, slower. It gave a satisfied *beep*.

He tugged the door open and rushed into the dimly lit foyer where the elevator's upper door stood closed. He slapped the key against the inner security pad next to it and brought the radio up at the same moment. "Try now!"

There was another awful silence, this one longer, but at least less crushing than the first. "We're... we're on the way. We're coming up."

"Are they in?" Derek asked from the door.

Caleb nodded and waved him forward. "Come on—get out of the rain. Anything we can do about securing this door? Just in case?"

Derek hurried to the keypad on the inside of the room. "The key card might lock it. But that could trap us in here."

It was a good point, and one that Caleb should have considered. He was scattered. Distracted. A dangerous combination.

How could he keep them all safe from the rain? If only—

The light cut out. The quiet grinding of the elevator stopped—a sound Caleb hadn't even noticed until it quit.

Derek pressed his back to the wall by the door. "They cut the power."

How long had it been? Thirty seconds? The elevator didn't take much longer than that to reach the surface. It was potentially just below them.

Liz's voice came over the radio. "Caleb! Caleb, can you hear me?"

"I'm here." He motioned to Derek. "Help me get the doors open."

Derek pushed his rifle around to his back and hustled to join Caleb at the door.

There was a hatch in the ceiling of the elevator. He'd seen it each time he'd taken it up to the surface and made a point of remembering. It would be too high for his wife or daughter to reach, but if one of them gave the other a knee to stand on, they could make it.

Caleb relayed his plan to his wife. "Let me know if the elevator changes direction. Look for the hatch on the ceiling. You or Lana boost the other up if you can't reach. Then climb out. Got that?"

"Copy that, Dad," Lana answered.

Derek tugged a knife free and slid it into the crack between the elevator doors. With a grunt, he levered it open enough to get their fingers in. Caleb pulled with all his effort on the right door and Derek on the left. They didn't come easily, but at last, the release triggered, and the doors eased open.

Derek shook out his hands. "They'll send men out the front to circle around."

Caleb agreed. It was the obvious thing to do. "Radio

Ray. Tell his people to expect it and keep them off us as long as they can."

Derek hesitated. "You sure they'll do it?"

"They want in," he pointed out. "They're not getting in unless they come through whoever comes out. They don't really have a choice."

Derek moved toward the open door and relayed the order while Caleb knelt by the elevator hatch.

"Liz!" he called down. "Lana! Can you hear me?"

"I'm out," Lana called back. Her voice sounded distant. They were further down than he'd hoped. "I'm getting Mom now."

"On the south wall," he told her, "opposite the door you came in, there will be rungs set into the wall. Use them to climb up."

He listened, peering down into the dark, and heard a grunt of effort. "Yeah," Lana called up. "Got them."

"Good. Come up as fast as you can but be careful."

"Oh, right! Thanks, I was going to—" A shock of thunder drowned out his daughter's last words, but Caleb smiled at the tone. If Lana could be a smart aleck, she wasn't so panicked that she couldn't function.

Liz might be another story, but she was with Lana— she always seemed to find her courage and composure when Lana was in sight.

"Come on," Caleb muttered, straining to see any movement in the elevator shaft or hear hands moving over steel rungs.

Outside, someone fired a shot. Then another. Short bursts of automatic fire.

"Contact," Derek called to him.

"I hear it," he called back, then leaned into the darkness, one hand gripping the edge of the elevator door. "Lana, how close are you? Can you see me?"

Her voice came up, much closer now, her breathing labored. "We can see light. Almost there... maybe... another ten yards."

Caleb looked back to the door. It was almost pitch dark outside now, making the flashlights mounted to the rifles the general's men carried stand out. Muzzles flashed in the distance from Ray and his people's direction. That was a small advantage, but the only place to take reliable cover was in this enclosure.

He turned to Derek. "Hold the door."

Derek didn't answer and didn't need to be told. Caleb's nerves were drawn tight, though, vibrating with adrenaline screaming to *do* something, to find the threat and neutralize it instead of waiting. But he couldn't pry himself away from the elevator shaft, either, for fear something would happen, and he wouldn't be there to prevent it.

"Incoming." Derek leaned forward and the room was briefly lit as he fired into the night.

Caleb inhaled, preparing to leave the elevator shaft and help Derek defend, when Lana's face came barely into view, a ghost rising from the darkness. He squatted down at the lip of the shaft and leaned to reach a hand out. "Almost there! Take my hand!"

Another couple of rungs, and Lana reached out and

took hold of his wrist. He closed his fingers around hers and pulled as he stood up to lift her out.

He hugged her briefly, squeezing her tight with a muttered, "Thank God you're safe," before she withdrew and gave him space.

He kneeled and reached for Elizabeth next. His hand closed around her wrist, and her fingers brushed his skin before she managed to grip his arm. With effort, he pulled her out and into his arms.

"I've got you," he rasped into her ear as he held her against him. "I've got you."

She trembled in his embrace, entire body shaking and shivering. He held her away from him, hands on her shoulders. "Are you okay?"

He couldn't see if she was hurt in the dark. His hands moved over her arms, to her sides, but she took them and held them steady.

"I'm okay," she assured him.

"Dad!" Lana shouted, and he turned to see her withdrawing from the door, a rifle in her hands. "Can we save the reunion?"

The fog of relief that had gripped Caleb dissipated. They weren't out of it yet. Not by a long shot. Sharp focus settled back into him, clearer and more intense now that he had his family in sight. He tugged Elizabeth away, and moved her to the wall, then to the corner inside the door. "Stay down and away from the door."

Elizabeth nodded as she crouched and pressed herself to the concrete.

Caleb moved to the edge of the door and knelt at

Lana's side, his rifle up as he tracked the moving lights outside. "We've got support. Some locals, out in the woods. They can't see us, so when they fire, get back behind cover. Derek? Toss me that radio."

Caleb caught it and lifted it to his mouth. "Ray, come in. You holding up? Got numbers on these people?"

It took a moment. "Jake here. Got some empty rifles. Ammo's not gonna last. Probably another dozen with lights, maybe others we can't see."

In the dark, a muzzle flashed for a full three seconds as someone sprayed fire wildly toward the general's men.

"Short bursts," Caleb shouted into the radio.

"Who are these people?" Lana asked as she leaned out and took a shot, then pulled back as bullets pinged against the outer wall.

"Not sure," Caleb admitted. "But they took out four patrol teams and were planning on invading the base."

Lana gave a snort. "And we're, what, on their team now?"

"Don't know that I'd call it that." Lightning flashed, lighting the open area between the door and the forest, illuminating a soldier without a light mounted to his rifle. Caleb looked down his sight and waited for the next burst of lightning. When it came, he homed in on the man, pulled the trigger twice.

No fire returned when the darkness swallowed everything again, but he hadn't seen the soldier go down.

He waited.

Derek eased back behind the wall. "They stopped."

Caleb frowned, listening to the darkness. There were

still shots being fired, but the muzzle flashes from the woods had gone dark. He took the radio up again. "Jake? What's happening?"

No answer. "Jake," he snapped, "respond."

Derek hissed a curse. "They took off. I *knew* they'd screw us. Redneck son of a—"

"Jake here," the radio hissed. "Y'all probably wanna take cover right about—"

Caleb didn't hear the rest as he yanked Lana back. His shout at Derek was swallowed up as three explosions lit the gloom.

CHAPTER TWENTY-ONE
LANA

Horse Creek Base, New United States
Friday, June 18th, 9:45 pm EST

Lana couldn't hear her heart beating or feel it in her body. Her bones ached, though, and her limbs felt like every vein had suddenly tried to eject their contents into her skin.

Something touched her face. Her instinct was to push it away—it was someone's hand, large enough to grip her entire jaw. There was some muffled sound, a kind of hoarse *whuff-whuff* that she felt along with a cough of warm air against her eyes.

Her eyes were closed, she realized. She opened them and her father's face loomed in her vision.

"Lana, look at me." This time she heard him.

"I'm okay," she told him, and pushed his hand away.

There was more light then, strobing in through the

door. The air vibrated with thunder that she barely heard but could feel in her chest and in the concrete under her. It lasted long enough that for a moment, she saw the room they were in was small, concrete, and covered in debris.

Her father's eyes roved over her face, down her neck, to her arm. Something had him worried, or maybe even terrified.

Oh, right.

She was still sticky with blood that had caked her face and arm from the guard at the elevator's entrance. Distantly, she felt like that should bother her, like she should be more concerned about it. Where that feeling should have been, though, there was only a blank spot—a numbness that refused to give up. She peered over her father's shoulder as Derek pushed himself to his feet unsteadily.

She grunted with effort and rolled up, accepting her father's hand to stand. The world shifted, tilting in an unexpected direction, and she braced herself on him.

"It'll pass." His voice still came muffled as if through wads of cotton in her ears.

Lana glanced around, found her mother leaning against the wall. She seemed dazed. Out of focus. She motioned toward her. "Help Mom," she told her father, and pushed past him to get to Derek.

"You okay?" Her hands searched first his shoulders, then his arms, then finally his hands. She squeezed. "Can you hear me?"

"All good," Derek replied. "Not my first concussion wave. You?"

"Dizzy," she admitted. "But it's already passing."

He gave her a rueful laugh. "Oh, just wait. It'll come and go for a few days."

Derek sagged against the wall, one hand still on hers. "That get 'em?"

She glanced at the darkened doorway and tried to listen for gunfire over the tinny sound in her ears. "Maybe." She turned back to him, still confused. "You're... I mean..." She frowned at the floor. "You're here."

His hand twisted beneath her fingers until their palms touched. "Yeah. I'm here. Your Dad... if he hadn't been there, if he hadn't fired first, I—"

She put her fingers over his lips, then leaned in and kissed him. It was brief, like before. But with none of the tension she'd felt that time. When she pulled back, his hand was tighter in hers. "I... there's blood on my face. Sorry."

"It's okay. I pissed myself about an hour ago. It's really cold."

A chuckle rose out of her, and she gave him a gentle shove. "Gross."

"It really is," he agreed.

Behind them, her father hissed for quiet.

Lana let Derek's hand go, all the humor of the moment vanishing as she twisted around and dropped to a knee. She didn't even notice pulling her rifle around, but it was in her hands, aimed at the dull rectangle of the open door that barely stood out in the dark.

There were footsteps outside, careful and cautious,

but still squishing in the soaked earth. She slipped her finger around the trigger and held her breath.

"Y'all alive in there?" someone whispered.

"Jake?" Caleb asked.

"All clear," Jake reported.

The rough, metallic rasp of a lighter sounded twice, and then there was an orange glow that lit the doorway. A man stepped through—not a soldier; or at least not one of General Thomas's people.

A weasely looking man, gaunt around the face, with uneven stubble on his jaw and lips, held a zippo in the air. He entered the enclosure and looked around.

The lighter's glow illuminated the small space and Lana found her father standing on the opposite side of the door, hood drawn and face grim, in front of her mother. He didn't look happy, but his rifle was at ease, at least. Lana lowered hers as well as she stood.

"You get your people?" the man wondered, his eyes tracking first Lana's mother, then her.

"Where's Ray?" Caleb asked, ignoring the question.

Another man pushed in, thicker in the jaw than the first. His hood was pulled too far forward to see much of him, but the set of his lips made it seem like he wasn't especially happy to see Caleb, or any of them, as he scanned the room. "So what we doing now? *Sir?*"

The way he said *sir*, thick with sarcasm, told Lana there was dangerous history there. But he did ask a legitimate question.

Caleb glanced at the elevator shaft. "Don't think we can get in this way. They cut the power. Brake's probably engaged. Even if we cut the cables, which we can't unless you've got some bolt cutters, and climbed down, it's sealed."

Lana's mother made a horrified sound. "Get *in*?"

"Dad, we can't go back in there," Lana began. "The whole place is on alert. The guys guarding the elevator knew something was up, said the general put an APB on us or something."

"Earth to you pansies, it's freakin' rainin' *acid* out here in case you ain't noticed. Any chance you wanna make room and let our boys inside?" Ray, probably, Lana thought. The way her father looked at him, she didn't think there were going to be introductions. The other man must have been Jake.

Caleb stepped aside to make space and met Lana's eyes. There was warning in them, and she shifted her grip on the rifle slightly, preparing herself to snap it up if needed, the way she'd practiced with Derek.

Other than the two she'd seen, six others filed in. It made the space crowded and claustrophobic and didn't leave any real room for maneuvering.

"You lost three?" Caleb asked, peering at the ragged group of men in hunting jackets. They ranged from one who was a head taller than him, to one that was barely as big as Lana's mother.

"Yeah, we lost three," Ray growled. "Three *friends*."

"You launched an assault on a military base," Caleb replied, his tone flat.

Lana cleared her throat. "And that was the *outside*.

Why do we want to go back in, again? Because that seems like a really bad idea."

"The rain," her mother offered. "Right?"

Caleb nodded. "We can't travel in this. The rain's acidic and freezing. According to sources," he nodded at Ray, "it can last for days. Without shelter, we'll freeze and burn all at the same time."

Lana thought about Maria back at the research facility, but one glance at the men crowding the room and she kept her mouth shut. If her father wasn't going to suggest it, he had a good reason.

The sky flashed, accompanied by thunder so immediately, it must have struck nearby. Lana's head swam and she blinked away white spots in her vision.

"How many soldiers were outside?" Derek asked.

Jake answered him. "Might have counted twelve, at least. Maybe more."

"Twelve flashlights?" Caleb asked. Jake gave him a nod, and Caleb considered for a moment. "I saw at least one with no light on... but it's better to overestimate. There were seven in our unit besides us. Four patrols, each of those were at least seven. Your boys took them all out?"

"Hell yeah, we did." Ray spat on the ground. "Fish in a barrel."

Derek took a step out from Lana's side. "All together, that's about three quarters of Thomas's military personnel. There are about another ten in civilian staff. Well, minus Lana and Eliz—er, Mrs. Machert. So, eight. All in all... that only leaves maybe twenty armed soldiers inside. Maybe less. The most ever here was eighty-eight."

Lana chewed the inside of her lip. Those odds were... better than she'd imagined. Her father seemed to think so as well, because he began to rub his jaw in the way that meant he was putting together a plan instead of deciding whether to go ahead.

Before Caleb could get his thoughts together, though, an idea blossomed in Lana's. "What were those explosives?"

The big man, the tallest of the lot, answered her. "TNT packed with pin nails."

Lana looked to Derek. "Any idea if the base's interior can take something like that?"

He shook his head. "I... don't know. Maybe?"

"Do you have any left?" she asked the big man.

He unzipped and opened his jacket, showing four white plastic tubes tucked into the inside. "Just a few."

Caleb frowned at her. "We can't use them inside the base. That blast wave from before was out in the open. We wouldn't survive it in a space that small."

Lana's lip curled at the corner. "I know. But if you'd just sent a bunch of people topside into a combat situation, and there was only one way into the base, you'd probably have it covered. Right?"

"She's right." Derek breathed out in a wave of excitement as he figured out Lana's line of thought. "The front elevator—it'll be under guard, probably. Not just outside. Probably... four at the door, four to six in the hall downstairs. But at that range, in that space—it wouldn't matter how many there were."

"How long are the fuses?" Caleb asked.

The big man glanced at him. "Ten-second burn. I got a little extra, could tie it on, pull the fuse from two of them... maybe thirty seconds? Forty? Hard to say."

Caleb nodded, then gave Lana a long, quiet look, his jaw flexing. "Okay. Then... Here's what we do..."

CHAPTER TWENTY-TWO
CALEB

Horse Creek Base, New United States
Friday, June 18th, 10:17 pm EST

"I ain't gettin' in no elevator with four of you'uns and two of us." Ray spat a glob of dip spit outside. "Don't seem fair to me."

"There's only cover for six." Derek began. "Anyone else will be slaughtered the second the doors open."

Ray crossed his arms.

Caleb's jaw ached from the tension radiating throughout his entire body. He practically hummed with it. "Liz—"

"If Lana goes, then I'm going." Her voice shook, her eyes watered, and she seemed about as confident as a mouse, but she was adamant. Whatever happened while they were escaping the base... It wasn't good.

He glanced at Lana and didn't even ask. *My little*

girl. He'd bounced her on his knee until she doubled over with giggles when she was two and taken on her first camping trip when she was only six. He'd taught her to fish and shoot and catch a baseball because she insisted baseball wasn't just for boys.

She'd snuggled up under his arm for twelve years until, one day, she was 'too old'. Then she'd gone to college, survived the apocalypse, and now stood in a concrete box with a pile of people, armed and covered in someone else's blood.

His little girl wasn't a *girl* anymore. Even after everything, he'd somehow held onto some feeling that she was still his, in some way. That they'd survive this and go camping again, and she'd make the fire but ask him to clean the fish because guts were gross. Or that she'd need to ask his advice about a boy, maybe.

But all of that was gone. He cleared his throat. Turned his voice hard. Cold. Unwavering. "We do this my way, or we don't do it at all." He stared Ray down. "Y'all can try your luck, blast that door open yourselves and get blown to pieces the second General Thomas's men catch sight of you, or you and Jake can come with us and have a chance."

He flicked his eyes toward Jake. "Your call."

It didn't take Ray long. He stepped outside and within a few minutes, four of Ray's men, including the big guy—Gun—slipped away into the night to circle around to the front of the base. Two others stayed up top at the back entrance to hold the line.

There were a lot of assumptions in this plan and

Caleb didn't like it. But he'd thought through the alternatives, and they were all worse. Lana had identified the one with the highest chance of success.

Lana. He glanced at his daughter. The light of the zippo lighter left open and burning on the floor cast shadows across her cheeks and almost hid the drying blood. *Almost.*

Elizabeth's fingers brushed the back of his hand and he turned to find her staring up at him. The flicker of light danced in her eyes and Caleb swore she understood all that floated and swirled in his head—this jumbled mess of love and fear and grim determination.

Now wasn't the time to work through it, though. Not when they needed to be focused. Not with *Ray* sharing the same oxygen. Caleb didn't like the man. Not the way he held himself, the way he looked at Caleb's rifle, and *especially* the way he glanced at Elizabeth and Lana both. If he was colder, he'd have taken Ray, Jake, and the two standing guard outside out as soon as he was sure the others were far enough away that they wouldn't hear the gunfire.

He needed the extra bodies, though. Someone to take a bullet that might otherwise be meant for Liz or Lana.

He shifted position and inhaled a slow breath. It was hard to say how long they waited in tense silence. Long past the last gasp of fuel in the zippo and the sputtering and dying of the flame. Long enough for the cold to settle into Caleb's body, leeching away warmth even through the heavy combat vest and the layers beneath it. Adrenaline and activity had kept him warm before. Standing around waiting for men he didn't trust didn't generate the same heat.

Sometime after the first shiver he couldn't control hit him, the radio crackled at his hip. "Machert." Gun's static-laden voice cut across the dark. "All clear."

Caleb exhaled slowly. The channel was set to 8.3 and should have been jammed. Masterson had restored the comms system, most likely by reloading the whole thing. There was a good chance that he'd pick up their chatter.

"Acknowledged," he replied into the radio. "We're coming in. Back elevator still inoperative. Let's go knock on the front door and see who answers."

"Roger that," Gun answered.

There was no way to know for sure that Masterson had picked up the communication, but the ploy was meant to be icing. The more men Thomas sent to the front elevator to wait, the better. He probably wouldn't leave himself isolated, of course, but at this point, he was running out of things to lose.

He put the radio back on his hip and shot a wary glance at Ray before turning to Elizabeth. He found her cheek with his hand and leaned down, brushing her lips with his. She pressed into him, teeth catching his lower lip for just a second.

He let the kiss go on a moment longer, then moved his mouth to her ear. "No matter what," he whispered, "you keep *behind* me. Understand?"

She nodded against his palm.

A short time later, the ground shuddered from a large explosion. Caleb crossed his fingers. If Gun and his men did it right, then the main elevator was now inoperable and the front entrance blocked. If the general wanted to deal with them, there was only one way now.

The light in the enclosure came on. *Bingo.* The elevator groaned to life. One by one, they withdrew from the room to wait on the other side of the open door. Caleb and Derek took one side, Ray and Jake took the other. Lana and Elizabeth waited behind, rain splattering their bare heads. If all went according to plan, the burns would be worth it.

Caleb raised his rifle and trained it on the elevator. When it finally opened, they painted the inside of it red.

CHAPTER TWENTY-THREE

Horse Creek Base, New United States
Friday, June 18th, 11:22 pm EST

Derek and Jake pulled the last of the bodies out of the elevator while Caleb, Lana, and the rest of them retrieved the rifles and any extra magazines. He stepped over the threshold and a memory came out of nowhere.

Lana, three years old, still chubby with baby fat, holding his index finger instead of his hand as they waited for elevator doors to open. A Christmas party, was it?

She bounced back and forth on the balls of her feet, waiting with anticipation. The elevator dinged, the doors slid open, and she hesitated at the precipice, little eyes straining to peer into the gap between the floor and the elevator. Caleb had lifted her up with one hand and swung her over the gap before picking her up to mash the button for the tenth floor.

When the elevator gave a lurch and began to rise, Lana's eyes had widened, and Caleb had watched with a smile he couldn't help as she bent her knees and bounced a little, exploring the strange change in her world caused by the inertia. The look on her face had been one of wonder, confusion, and delight. *Magic.*

He watched her now, face sober and grim at the opposite corner of the elevator. No magic. No wonder. Only iron determination and white knuckles.

"Relax your grip," he told her. "Try not to tense up."

She glanced at him and nodded before shifting a bit on her feet. Her shoulders lowered and her knuckles regained some color. Her chest rose and fell in a slow and deep breath, and she focused, just like he'd done so many times before a conflict.

Had he made her that? Or had she just adapted to the circumstances?

The elevator slowed and he shoved his thoughts—of Lana, Elizabeth, even his concern about Ray and Jake—out of his mind. It was do or die in the next few moments. *Go time.*

"Anyone in fatigues." Caleb spoke to the group as a whole. "Anyone with a weapon in hand. There are unarmed civilians inside as well, so keep your eyes sharp."

"Yes, sir," Derek replied.

The others just gave various grunts and nods of understanding.

They pressed themselves to the sides of the elevator, just barely covered by the narrow walls on either side of the inner door. The compartment settled with a rattling jerk. The doors opened slowly.

An awful smell flooded the elevator immediately, and Caleb's eyes took in a floor stained with dark, greasy-looking liquid that had streaks dragged through it where bodies had been moved. He tipped forward enough to get a quick look around the door.

There were men at the end of the hall. Some standing, some kneeling. They'd stacked crates and boxes to make a barricade for cover. But they didn't immediately fire, even though they'd had to have seen him peeking out.

"What are they waiting for?" Elizabeth whispered.

Caleb shook his head. He didn't know. Maybe they were worried about damaging the only exit from the base that was left?

Ray had the front spot on the other side of the elevator and cast him a look of suspicion. "Somebody's gotta take the first shot," he growled.

Before Caleb could weigh whether that was true, the general's voice came over the intercom speaker in the hallway. "Staff Sergeant Machert. This is General Thomas. You have one chance to stand down and turn yourself over. Do so, and your family will be safe. You have my word."

"He's lying," Lana whispered.

Yes, he probably was. But the fact that he was playing

any kind of game at all meant that he was nervous. He knew how few men he had left.

Caleb glanced at Derek, his voice low. "Anyone else here have doubts about the general's methods?"

Derek met his eyes, and his lips thinned, but his face remained uncertain.

Maybe every soldier left was a fanatic. But maybe they weren't—and if all they were was afraid, then they didn't deserve to die, or to live under a madman.

One way to find out. "Listen to me," Caleb called into the hallway ahead of them. "Whatever you think General Thomas is going to accomplish here, whatever he's told you, it's not the truth."

He took a deep breath. "Topside, it's nothing but freezing acid rain. The soil won't grow food for years, the surrounding towns that aren't flattened are going to be picked clean. The coast is unlivable, people are fleeing west. More and more people."

He glanced at Derek. "Are you really prepared to keep killing every civilian coming this way who General Thomas deems unworthy?"

There was no response, but he hadn't expected it right away. They needed to hear it, sit in it.

"Ask yourself this," he went on. "What kind of nation are you going to make with corpses? What kind of *New* United States can you build on ash and poisoned soil? And who are you going to be when he's done with you?"

Derek shifted behind him, and Caleb raised his voice even louder. "I get it—this base feels like safety and structure that we all lost when the rock hit us. It seems like an island of order in all this chaos. But it's not."

He glanced at Elizabeth with a grim smile. "The only thing I want in the world is to keep my family safe, and when we got here, I was willing to look past my own doubts because I *needed* this place to be a shelter for them. I needed to feel like I was doing something; like I was getting the job done. But that's not what this place is. It's a grave."

He wished he could see even one soldier's face to know if he was getting through. "If we stay here, if we let the general bury us, body and soul, that's what it will be for us. You don't have to follow him. He's not the king he wants to be. Not yet. Not unless you make him one."

He waited almost a minute.

The general's voice came over the intercom again. "That's a nice speech, Machert. But your time's up. Lay down your weapons and come out with your hands up, or my men open fire."

He looked to Lana and his wife. Both shook their heads. They were in it together. "We're not doing that," Caleb called. "This only ends one way."

"Very well. Light 'em up."

All six of them tensed, pressing to the walls of the elevator. The *crack-crack* of automatic burst-fire filled the hallway. But no bullets struck the back wall of the elevator or the walls outside.

When it was quiet, Caleb leaned out to grab a quick snapshot of the scene. It took a moment to process before he leaned out again more slowly.

At the end of the hall, behind the barricade, there were fewer soldiers. Two of them had their rifles raised—but not at the elevator. One of them met Caleb's eyes, then lowered his weapon. The other remaining man did the same, and from around the corner another stepped into view, his rifle lowered.

"I didn't join the Army to kill civilians," one of them shouted.

Caleb closed his eyes with a sigh of relief. "I know you didn't," he replied, and moved to step out.

Ray hissed at him, face twisting with incredulity as Elizabeth grabbed Caleb's arm to pull him back.

"You crazy?" Ray demanded.

"Caleb," Elizabeth whispered, her eyes wide with the same uncertainty. "It could be a trap."

"I don't think—" Caleb started.

Before he could finish, Derek stepped away from the wall, rifle hanging from the strap, his hands raised. Lana made a choked noise and flinched toward him, but he stepped away from her and to the door. "We don't have to be what he wants to make us."

After a few seconds of standing in the open, Derek lowered his hands. His face was white. His eyes twitched toward Caleb, and he gave a shallow nod before he stepped out of the elevator entirely.

Caleb watched him go, then tugged gently out of Elizabeth's grip and went out after him. One by one, the others filed out.

The men at the end of the hall came forward, stepping around the barricade. All of them had wariness written on their features, their eyes rimmed with dark circles. Though cautious, they met Caleb as he took the lead in front of Derek to approach them.

"What are your names?"

"Private Colby Anders," the first one said.

"Private Charles Mulaney," another answered.

"Private Willis Washington," the final one said. "Army Reserve. There's a six-man detail in the situation room, sir, and two more pinch points at the west and north corridors, both barricaded, two men each."

Caleb nodded, surveying the three men, then looking past them to the splayed bodies behind the barricade. He frowned and searched the eyes of the three soldiers. "I'm sorry."

Private Anders swallowed hard and focused on the wall behind him. The other two gave slow, grim nods. None of them wanted to be here, killing civilians *or* fellow soldiers.

"We offer everyone the chance to stand down," he told them. "Anders, Washington—you two find any civilian staff you can and make sure they're secured and out of danger. Mulaney, any idea if there are more men topside?"

"Don't think so. Not that I've heard. Thomas gave the order to withdraw and secure the situation room and the corridors leading to it when the... the bomb went off."

All according to plan. Caleb motioned toward the elevator. "You head back up. Stay covered when you get there and tell the two men topside you're with Ray, and that you need to get the survivors inside and out of the rain. Head south of the elevator, keep your hands off your rifle and in the air, and tell them Staff Sergeant Machert gave the all-clear."

"Sir?" Mulaney asked. "You sure you want to bring them into this?"

"It's raining acid and close to freezing. There are kids. They can't be out in this any longer. By the time you get them down here, we'll have this place cleared."

Ray snorted. "You can't be serious. You can't just bring a bunch of—"

Caleb rounded on him, quieting the man with a look. "This isn't a discussion."

Ray fell silent, a scowl turning his features even uglier.

Caleb looked over the group. "Let's move in. Slow and careful."

They waited for the elevator to close, then filed around the corner with Anders and Washington on point. At the end of the hallway, the two privates peeled off and headed toward the north end of the base to carry out Caleb's orders, and he brought Ray up to lead point with him.

The six of them reached the first pinch point within a few minutes, and Caleb glanced around the corner to find a barricade set up just like Private Washington warned him. The concrete near his face exploded as they fired, and he jerked back to avoid the spray or a bullet. When the fire paused, he offered them the same chance he had the others. "You don't want to live in the world he wants to make."

Derek didn't step out this time. Neither did Caleb. He knelt and checked again and got only another round of fire in response.

Ray spat. "So much for the great leader speech."

Caleb ignored the man. "Get me some cover fire."

"Gladly," Ray muttered.

Derek pressed forward. "I'll go low."

The two of them inched to the corner, and after a short count, both swung their rifles around and fired down the corridor.

Caleb sucked in a breath and dropped to a knee as he moved into view. One of the men popped up briefly, then appeared to the side of the barricade, training the barrel of his weapon on Caleb. Caleb snapped his aim to the side and down and fired twice.

A burst of powdered concrete plumed into the soldier's face and the second shot took him in the cheek. He fell back. The other man came up firing over the top of the barricade.

Caleb threw himself sideways, his finger locked on the trigger. The last rounds in his clip emptied in the soldier's direction. One of them took him in the chest, but only after a searing line of fire burned across Caleb's upper thigh.

Derek broke cover a split second after, keeping low as he stalked down the corridor. He reached the barricade and fired again. "All clear."

"Caleb!"

Elizabeth pushed past Lana, who tried to get a hold

on her mother, and rushed to Caleb's side as he began to stand. "You're hit."

His thigh burned as he put weight on it, but it didn't buckle. He took Liz's shoulder to keep her upright when she moved to check his wound. "Just grazed," he assured her. "Stay in the back, I don't want you—"

"Get down!"

Two more men emerged from the far end of the corridor. The team from the other route to the Situation Room. The wall behind them exploded as bullets struck concrete, pelting Caleb's shoulder and back with jagged shards as he plowed into his wife and hurled them out of the line of fire. Before they struck the floor, something hot struck his left calf.

He and Liz went down hard even as he tried to catch himself with an arm and keep her from slamming onto the floor. His arm buckled as he twisted, and his shoulder crashed into the concrete with a loud, wet crunch. Another burst of agony blossomed across his upper body.

He ignored it, rolling to cover Liz with his body. There was a short chaos of shouting and gunfire. Pain radiated from his calf, from his thigh, from this shoulder, all coalescing into a searing throb. Liz's breath came hot and labored against his neck, and she flinched at every renewed round of fire.

At some point, it was over, gunfire replaced by his wife's sobs.

"It's okay," he whispered hoarsely, and pressed his cheek to hers. "It's okay, you're okay. Lana?"

"Here," Lana called, "I'm here—*oh, no!* Derek!"

Before Caleb tried to push himself up, Derek and Lana were on him, pulling him off his wife. His shoulder screamed as he rolled over it, and he barely managed to contain a howl of pain. White spots filled his vision as he grit his teeth and tempered the sound down to a pained growl.

"Here." Derek handed Lana his knife.

Liz pushed herself up to kneel at Caleb's side and her face paled as she looked him over.

He started to rise.

"Stay still," Lana ordered. "Mom, keep him down."

"I'm fine," Caleb insisted, but Liz put a hand on his chest.

"No, you're not."

Lana tugged at his leg, and the muscle there contracted, sending a flood of fresh, torturous sensation through Caleb's body, straight to his stomach. Fabric ripped, and Lana handed the knife back to Derek. "Looks like it went clean through," she said. "Dad... just... keep still."

He nodded, his breath suddenly harder to get into his chest, and braced himself for what he knew was coming. Lana's hands moved over his bare leg, wrapping something around it. She gave a grunt, and a jolt of pain shot up again as she tightened a tourniquet down over the wound.

Caleb gasped as she tightened it twice more, then pinned his leg down and tied it off. "That'll have to hold for now. Dad? Mom is he—"

"I'm here." Caleb grasped at Liz's hand. He held it tight and nodded up at her. "Help... help me up."

She hesitated, but then Lana was in view and taking his other arm. They pulled him upright and he saw the ugly mess of his leg for the first time and the smeared pool of blood. It was a lot, but not so much that he felt cold. The bullet had gone through his muscle and missed the tibial artery.

It was bad, but not the end. Not if they could finish this and get it treated properly in the next hour or so. "Help me stand," he told them.

"No, Dad," Lana said, "you shouldn't walk on it, we can go ahead."

He shook his head. "Not letting the two of you walk in there without me," he growled, and held Lana's arm tight when she tried to pull away. He gave her a firm, serious look. "I've been shot before. We do this together. Get me up."

She glanced at her mother as if looking for permission. Liz hesitated. "Caleb..."

Ray stepped forward, and held a hand out. There was a half-smirk on his face that Caleb didn't like, but he took the man's hand and ground his teeth again as he strained with his injured shoulder to sit up. The pain nearly blinded him.

"Just a scratch," Ray said, smiling as he clapped Caleb on the injured shoulder. "Ain't that right?"

Caleb would have decked him if he could. Instead, he focused on Derek. "Take point. Situation room. We don't stop until it's done. Thomas has to go."

"Yes, sir," he agreed.

Lana moved to join him, but Caleb reached out to stop her. "No, Lana you—*shit*."

Liz slipped under his good shoulder before he could topple. His injured leg wouldn't take even the weight of shifting forward. He steadied himself, shifted his weight to his heel, and kept his calf as relaxed as he could.

"I'm alright." He brushed Elizabeth's hand away. "I can walk, just have to be careful."

"Dad," Lana said evenly, "you can barely hold your rifle. We can't go back, you said it yourself. I can *do* this."

He'd have argued with her, and almost did—but she turned away and joined Derek, and there wasn't much he could do about it. He sighed and shifted the strap of his rifle up and over his head. "Take this." He held it out to his wife. "Give me your sidearm. Your gun."

Her lips tight, she accepted the rifle and slid the strap over her head to rest on her shoulder, then pressed the pistol into his hand, her fingers closing over his as he gripped it. "Don't get yourself killed," she warned him.

Caleb glanced at Ray, who was still eyeing him like a vulture waiting for an animal to die. "I won't," he promised. *I'll never leave the two of you alone with this man.*

"Everyone ready? Check your ammo. One more to go."

Derek nodded. Lana watched him a moment longer and then looked away. At Caleb's order, they moved ahead together.

CHAPTER TWENTY-FOUR
LANA

Horse Creek Base, New United States
Friday, June 18th, 11:51 pm EST

Lana's pulse raced. Adrenaline coursed through her, burning and vibrating in every limb. The ground felt more solid under the soles of her boots, as if it pushed against her each time she took a step. Her skin seemed to register every contact with the fabric of her fatigues, and the rifle in her hands felt lighter than it should have been.

She knew that she should have been afraid. She should have been anxious, at least. Instead, there was a hard-edged numbness filling her up, swallowing everything until she was made entirely of focus and cold purpose.

"Door'll be secured."

When she didn't respond, Derek slowed, prompting her to glance at him in question. "You okay?"

"Just want to get this over with." She didn't like the way his brow furrowed, or the pinch at the corners of his eyes registered concern. "Keep moving," she prodded.

He looked away, and together they led the group to the final corner. Derek checked it, signaled them forward, and she rounded it with him.

A short corridor led to the white-painted door of the situation room. The camera blister above blinked slowly. The general was watching.

Derek approached the door and pressed the key card to the pad beside it. It gave a negative buzz, the light flashing red. He shrugged. "Worth a shot."

"What's the alternative?" Lana asked.

"Blow the security pad out." He glanced past her to where her father stood leaning against the wall to take weight off his injured leg.

A trail of blood followed behind him. That, at least, brought some emotion into Lana's numbness. She had to remind herself that the bullet hadn't nicked an artery. If they made it through this, he could be fixed up. If they didn't... Well, then it wouldn't matter.

Some part of her wanted to go to him, and her mother, hug them, and share some final words, just in case. But the weight of that blank feeling pressed back against her, tightening down. If she broke now, she might not be able to put herself back together.

Caleb waved at Jake. "Give me your radio."

Jake tugged it from where it was clipped at the back of his pants to hand it over.

Caleb twisted the dial, then spoke into it. "General Thomas, I'm asking you to stand down."

There was a brief silence before the intercom crackled to life. "What makes you think I would do that, Machert?"

Was that resignation in his voice?

"You're out of people," Caleb replied. "The situation room has one way in or out. There are armed civilians already in the base now. You can open now, or we can post guards out here and wait for you to starve. The supplies will keep us fed for a while. If that's what we have to do, that's what we'll do."

"And then what, Machert?" Thomas asked. "You want to take my place? You think you can lead these people?"

"No." Caleb shook his head. "I'm not going to lead anyone. I don't know if a man like you can believe this, General, but I'm in this for two reasons. My wife, and my daughter. You're a threat to them. That's all. To be honest, I barely care if you want to carve out some kingdom for yourself here. But you threatened my family, and you've killed a lot of people. *You're* the chaos, General."

There was another long silence, broken only by a distant rumble of thunder that Lana felt more than heard. With it, though, came a flicker of the lights.

"Corporal Masterson," Caleb spoke into the radio. "You're on comms?"

There was no answer.

"I know you are. I know you're listening. I'm betting

everyone in there can hear me. We can end this peace-fully, with as little bloodshed as possible. Turn the general over, and we can all live—"

There was a single gunshot over the intercom.

Caleb closed his eyes and lowered the radio.

"You're not poisoning any more of my people, Machert," the general growled over the intercom. "You want me? Come on in. Let's see what your naive idealism is worth."

The keypad flashed green, and the door gave a deep *thunk* as the lock disengaged.

Derek reached for the handle, glanced back at Caleb, and waited for a signal.

Lana's gut twisted. Anxiety finally reached her, clawing at her insides. A flash of insight burst into her thoughts. The gunshot had sounded over the intercom.

Not from behind the door.

Caleb gave Derek a nod. Lana surged forward and grabbed Derek's arm. "Don't, it's a—"

She didn't hear the explosion. One second, she was at the door, prying Derek's hand away from the handle, and the next she was on the ground, the air crushed from her lungs. Her vision tunneled, light cutting in and out. Her whole body throbbed. She scraped her hands over the floor, clawing for purchase to move, to get up, to try and react, do *anything*, but her body refused to move with any urgency.

With an effort that made her head pound, she craned her neck. Everything doubled, her vision wobbling. The security door was bent at two corners, but still mostly intact.

"Mom?" she tried to say. "Dad?"

Her words came out slurred. She managed to twist her body to one side and roll to her stomach. She got a hand under her. On wobbly arms, she pushed herself up to her knees. Ray and Jake were in sight, groaning as they tried to stand. She didn't see her parents, or Derek, and hot, fresh panic bubbled up inside.

Someone coughed behind her, and she twisted to find Derek on his back. One arm was bent at the wrong angle, and blood matted the hair on the side of his head. His other arm, opposite her, made confused, jerky movements. He coughed again, and blood spattered his lips.

Jessup's face swam in her vision.

"No," she breathed, and clambered toward Derek. "No, no, no—you can't—"

His eyes focused on her. He licked his lips. "Kay," he rasped. "S'okay... g-get... security room... only other place... intercom..."

Derek's eyes rolled. He coughed again and more blood flecked his lips.

Her father's voice called from behind her. "Lana!"

She tore herself away from Derek. "Dad, I'm here."

Caleb emerged from around the corner, her mother with him. They'd been behind cover when the trap had sprung. Caleb leaned heavily on the wall. "Derek?"

Lana shook her head and staggered, a wave of vertigo and nausea forcing her to stop. "He—I don't know. He's breathing."

"We've got to move."

Her father was right. They couldn't stay there and wait for the general's remaining men to come mop them up. She looked back at Derek. They couldn't leave him. Not again—not like they'd left Jessup.

"He's in the security room," Lana said, turning to face her father. "It's the only other place to access the intercom system."

Caleb bared his teeth in a grimace and cursed. "It's not far. Come on."

He turned to go, limping a step away.

"We can't just leave him," Lana called after him.

Caleb stopped and turned back to her. He opened his mouth to speak but nothing came out.

"I'll stay with him," Elizabeth offered. Caleb watched her as she came toward Lana and knelt beside Derek. "I'm... I'll just be in the way."

Lana stared at her, unsure what to say.

Her mother reached out and put a hand to her arm, holding her gaze. "I promise, it won't be like Jessup."

Grief and fear coiled around Lana's chest and constricted until she could barely breathe. But a moment later, her mother's hand reached her cheek, her palm warm and rough. "Go keep your father safe."

It took an effort of will, but Lana stood slowly, watched Derek's chest rise and fall once, then twice, and finally stepped back. "We'll be back," she told her mother. "Both of us."

Elizabeth smiled at her, and then at Caleb, and gave a nod. "I know. You make a good team."

Lana bit her lip as she withdrew and joined her father, offering her shoulder to lean on. Jake and Ray joined them, both limping, faces pinched with pain.

"We're going to come back," Caleb promised Lana softly.

"Yeah," she agreed as they checked and turned a corner, "I know."

CHAPTER TWENTY-FIVE
CALEB

Horse Creek Base, New United States
Saturday, June 19th, 12:36 am EST

It was dangerous to run on anger. Caleb knew that; knew that it would make him irrational, screw with his judgment, make him prone to mistakes that could cost him dearly. But it was the only thing that kept the pain in his leg and shoulder at bay. It didn't do a good job, but it certainly made it easier to force himself to take step after step.

He'd underestimated General Thomas. He wouldn't do it again, but it felt like the damage had been done. It was easy to tell Lana that they'd get back to her mother and to Derek. It was harder to make himself really believe it.

Even if they did pin Thomas down in the security room, he didn't know that he could take a clear shot in his condition. The general wasn't going to stand down. Offering the out had been the right thing to do, though.

So, good for him. If he died here, he could die with a clear conscience. If he didn't...

What if the world is too dangerous to do the right thing anymore?

Maybe it was the loss of blood, and the exhaustion that he was barely keeping from swallowing him up, but he couldn't keep the thought away. Who would he be —*what* would he be—if he set aside his principles over and over to keep his family safe? Worse—what would they become if he let them follow him down that path?

He looked sidelong at Lana as they limped toward the final turn in the corridor ahead. She'd killed someone. She'd killed a few people now, of course, but... she only got that bloody by killing someone up close, with her hands.

A knife, probably; she and Derek had been doing a lot of knife work, and Caleb had taught her some himself. He was sure that she'd had to do it. It was survival—her or someone else, and he'd have chosen her *every* time, whatever the circumstances were.

But it did mean she was changed. All of this had changed her. She was fluid now, still transforming into whatever she'd need to be to make it through this, if there was even a way through to be found. If he stopped doing 'the right thing', if he showed her that it was okay to give up principles to survive...

Would it be his fault if she lost her center—her goodness?

What was worse, though, was the burning desire to tell her all of this while there was time. That he'd wanted to be a moral man. That if there was any other choice, they wouldn't be hunting Thomas down to kill him. That she needed to stay good and true and not let the ugly bits of the new world ruin her.

But if he told her even a snippet of his thoughts, she might hesitate. And that might get her killed.

Lana slipped from under his arm carefully, giving him a chance to catch his balance, and slid along the wall to the corner. She readied her rifle, and leaned out briefly to check, pulling back too quickly for anyone with normal reflexes to get a shot at her. Almost a professional.

"That's the door." She peered around the corner again, this time longer. "There are voices. Can't make them out clearly."

Above them, another earth-shaking boom of thunder sounded. The lights in the corridor flickered, then dimmed.

Then, they went out.

The darkness was absolute and instant.

Jake hissed out a curse.

Caleb held an arm out. "Lana?"

Fabric brushed his fingers. Her hand found his and she maintained contact with his arm. "I'm here. Dad—the lock disengaged. I heard it shut down. It'll lock again when the backup power comes on."

He tried to get his fingers around her hand. "We can't go in—*no,* Lana wait—"

But she'd already pulled away. *No!*

He waved frantically in the darkness, choking down her name when he almost shouted it. He felt for the wall and got his hand on it, then limped forward, following it to the corner. "Ray," he whispered, "Jake. Quiet as you can. Straight ahead. Be ready."

He felt them shuffle past him and eased around the corner. He half fell to one knee and raised his weapon with his good arm.

There was a whisper of sound when the door opened, but it was enough for him—and it was enough for the people inside.

"Down!" someone inside called.

Rifles fired. The darkness was interrupted by strobing orange flashes. Caleb's heart leaped to his throat, but he saw Lana pressed against the wall by the door. He aimed at one of the flashing muzzles and fired. Three shots. The strobing paused, then picked up again, showing Lana on one knee, leaning around the doorway.

Lana took two shots. The strobing stopped, then started—shorter and briefer this time. He saw the two hunters on their knees, rifles up as they fired into the darkened room.

Backup lights came on—weak and red, flickering slightly.

Lana took another shot, and then slipped into the room. Panic flooded Caleb's body, driving him forward to go after her.

"You f-ing crazy?" Ray barked behind him.

The words barely registered. His daughter was going to die. He staggered through the doorway to find her gunning down one man while another whirled with his weapon raised.

"Here!" Caleb shouted, the sound explosive in his chest, scraping at his throat. He brought his pistol up as the man flinched and trained his rifle on Caleb.

He pulled the trigger. The man spun. Not a kill shot, but enough to throw off his aim. The man's rifle flashed and the shot went wide. Another shot from behind Caleb and the soldier fell backward. Ray and Jake were at the door now, picking men off—all but General Thomas.

Thomas was crouched down, barely visible behind a toppled file cabinet. Lana sprayed the cabinet with fire, advancing a step at a time toward him. Until her rifle clicked, empty.

Caleb's lungs seized. Every moment he'd watched his little girl over the years, full of parental worry—first teetering steps, first time climbing a jungle gym, first time off a diving board—every rush of a heartbeat and a held breath, hoping she would learn and grow and thrive. It hit him all at once.

Caleb raised his gun. The general surged out of cover, his sidearm coming up. Lana was in the open, an easy target. Caleb's leg buckled, and he dropped sideways, firing.

One shot lodged in Thomas's hip. He spun, stumbled toward the wall, and fell as he tried to catch himself. He hit the ground, weapon still clutched in his grip, and roared as he aimed it at Caleb.

But the shot that cracked the air jerked General Thomas's head back. His fingers twitched once, then went still. Lana stood a few feet away, rifle from a fallen soldier aimed down at him.

As Caleb watched, she lowered it, swallowed so hard her head bobbed, and closed her eyes. Her shoulders rose and fell.

She stood for a long moment before she finally forced her feet to move and came toward Caleb.

"Okie-dokie." Ray stepped fully into the security room. "Guess that fixes that."

"It's done," Lana said, her voice flat. "We need to get back to Mom."

"Well," Ray said slowly, training his rifle casually on Lana. "Not *quite* done. Thing is, we *did* come here to take this base, and way I see it, it's ours now, so I'm thinking you two are just about—"

Between the sudden silence, the fury that rose in Caleb's chest, and the fear at seeing Lana in the man's sights, the gunshot that exploded Ray's face from behind made Caleb bark with surprise.

Ray hung in the air, life draining his body for a long moment before he dropped lifeless to the floor. Jake stood behind him, wide-eyed as he lowered his weapon.

Caleb blinked at him, wary, his finger itching at the trigger of his gun. Lana stood perfectly still, her rifle half-raised.

Jake sagged against the doorway. "Bastard," he rasped, and finally looked up from his dead friend. "I never did trust him, but I didn't know. I promise, I didn't."

"It's okay." Caleb reached for Lana. She helped him

to his feet, and he limped to the door, stepping over Ray as he did. He gave Jake a long look. "Thank you."

Jake's jaw quivered. He dipped his head in a jerky motion as he stared at Ray. "He's got a girl back home." His voice rang hollow. "Two boys, too."

Caleb looked down at the fallen man. It was hard to imagine him as a husband or a father. "Will they miss him?"

Jake's brow knit and his lips turned hard. "I guess they probably won't."

"Then make sure you're a better man than he is. Do we need to worry about your other friends?"

"No," Jake assured him. "No, I'll... I'll get 'em sorted."

Caleb nodded. "When we're gone, you can keep the base if you want it. We're not staying."

"Come on," Lana murmured. She slipped under Caleb's arm, and together they left Jake standing in the room alone.

CHAPTER TWENTY-SIX
LERLAINE

Bartow Hill Road, Lansing, NC
Saturday, June 19th, 11:50 am EST

Lerlaine cringed as another boom of thunder shook the trailer. The wind howled constantly. The rain came down in sheets, drips of it leaking through a patch in the roof that Ray had probably done himself. Pressed against her chest, Hunter shrieked, his infant lungs pumping as he cried so hard, he'd be hoarse before long—a stuttering wail that rose and fell the same way the rain seemed to as the wind whipped it against the side of the trailer.

Maddox was just as bad, clinging to her leg, his face red and wet. She tried to comfort him. She tried to comfort them both. But there was no soothing them when it seemed like the whole world was shaking. When the sky opened and delivered God's fury.

Two days. Ray had been gone for two days. Of

course, he hadn't said how long it would take. But she'd gotten a feeling in her gut that he wasn't coming back. That no one was. It had been a suicide run for all of them, some kind of last-ditch effort to *do* something when it seemed like there was nothing to do. She'd had plenty of time to think about it, process it. Realize what kind of blind desperation was really driving Ray, and probably the others.

That had always been Ray. Desperation, alcohol, and the delusion that you could hit, scream, or cuss at any problem and it would just go away. That everything would fall in line. People, appliances, problems—to Ray, they were all the same.

She'd fantasized about making it work here, without him. But the generator was almost out of fuel. And this storm...

The rain and the wind and the lighting... If the wind kept up, the walls would crumble all around them. A bigger storm would pick up the trailer and drag it piecemeal down the hill. An earthquake would flatten it.

They couldn't stay. She knew that. Except, this time, she didn't have even a miserable little trailer to take her children to.

So, what was it, then? Stay there, get buried in debris and burned by the rain, only to freeze to death out in the open? Or take the only chance she had left?

Make a real leap of faith.

The cries of her sons seemed like they'd split her eardrums. She heard them over the loudest explosions of thunder. Nothing drowned them out, nothing gave her any relief. She sat, stunned by it all and paralyzed by a decision that seemed... Well, it didn't seem like a decision at all.

It felt like choosing how they died. How she watched her children die, because they were young, and fragile, and she wasn't in her prime, maybe, not after everything, but she would probably still live just long enough.

After a while, the rain let up. Not entirely, and the wind still buffeted the sides of the trailer and rattled the windows. The thunder and lightning still tore out of the sky. But the solid sheets of rain were the most dangerous part of it. If she had a window, it might be very narrow. She had to decide.

"Alright, baby." She pried Maddox from her leg. "Listen—get your coat, okay? And your boots and... I'll get you some gloves. Wait right here, alright?"

Maddox didn't seem to comprehend, but if she had to, she'd just bundle him up herself. She went to the bedroom and grabbed the keys to Ray's car from the top of the dresser and tucked them into the front left pocket of her jeans.

Calm settled on her. Maybe just doing *something* actually did make a person feel somehow more in control, even when they weren't.

She moved to the kitchen and fished a trash bag from under the sink. She shook it out with one hand, shushing Hunter as she did. "*Sh, sh, sh*, honey bear," she crooned with forced sweetness, "it's okay. It's okay, baby. Mama's here. Mama's gonna keep you safe and sound. *Sh, sh, sh*."

There was no point in discriminating about food, so

she pulled everything from the cabinets that she could find. Boxed stuff she'd have to figure out a way to rehydrate and cook. A meager assortment of canned food. The can opener. Venison steaks and sausage in the freezer. Jerky in the fridge.

It felt laughably inadequate, and poorly planned. Like she was six years old again, stuffing a pillowcase with toys and candy in preparation to run away. The thought caught her, grabbed her attention, and held it.

For a few seconds, she remembered the feel of the stretchy, printed cotton in her fingers, the weight of her improvised sack, and the way the toys poked at her belly when she held it tight. She stood on the porch of the shack she lived in with her mother back then, thinking that she had everything she needed to make a life for herself somewhere far away.

She was so very, very wrong.

Thunder boomed and brought her out of it. She stared down at the bag. This was the same, wasn't it?

But it didn't change anything. She knelt, and with one hand, collected the ties of the bag and drew them together with a jerk, then hefted the heavy load over her shoulder and went to the front door to put it down.

It took a few more minutes to get Hunter swaddled enough to keep the stinging rain off him, and another few to wrangle Maddox into his coat and boots and a pair of gloves that were too big for him while he continued to cry himself raspy and snotty and pathetic.

When She was satisfied that they were covered, she covered her own head with one of Ray's wide fishing hats and brought Maddox to the front door. She gathered her oldest son up into her arm to saddle her hip, then knelt to catch the trash bag with her hand.

Laden like some beast of burden, Lerlaine pawed at the door to get it open, took a breath as if she were diving into deep waters, and rushed out to the covered car.

It wasn't easy to uncover it. The trash bag had to be dropped, and was instantly muddy and soaked. She had to set Maddox down to free her hand, and his crying grew louder as the cold and the freezing, stinging rain splashed what little skin was exposed.

Already, she was failing.

Lerlaine worked as quickly as she could with only one arm, and in a short time, the old, low-riding car was exposed, its once bright blue and red paint long faded, the body rusted in places from long disuse.

Ignoring the state of the vehicle, she unlocked the doors and tucked Maddox inside, and put Hunter on his lap. "You hold onto your baby brother," she told him. "Understand?"

She hadn't been able to bring the car seat. But she buckled them in and stuffed the trash bag of supplies into the trunk by the large speakers Ray had installed there. And then, when she didn't think she could make any of it any safer, she finally tugged open the driver's door, slipped inside, closed her eyes, and turned the key in the ignition. She prayed Ray had kept the car at least in drivable condition.

The engine sparked, caught, and growled to life. Lerlaine's relief came out in a sudden, joyous sob. Just the one, before she pressed her forehead to the steering wheel, smiling through quiet tears to indulge in a moment of unfettered gratitude to God, or the universe, or whoever was responsible for seeing her and her children this far. Maybe—just *maybe*—someone really was looking out for them.

She put the car into drive, released the parking brake, and eased it away from the trailer. *Not safe yet,* she reminded herself, eyeing a gas gauge only half-full, *but at least we have a chance.*

If whoever was watching over her and her children kept an eye out just a little while longer, though, maybe a chance was all she needed.

CHAPTER TWENTY-SEVEN
ELIZABETH

Horse Creek Base, New United States
Saturday, June 19th, 4:10 pm EST

The storm lasted the better part of two days. Elizabeth spent them at Caleb's side. In a perfect world, he'd probably have gotten surgery for his shoulder. As it was, the best they could manage was a sling from medical and to position it so it would heal with a chance of functioning again

One of the survivors Caleb and Derek saved out on the mountain was a physical therapist before the disaster. She did what she could to get him positioned correctly. Willis—Private Washington—had enough field medic training to get Caleb's leg wound cleaned and stitched.

After that, Caleb had gone to sleep and mostly stayed that way.

When the thunder stopped, and Lana reported that

the rain had cleared, Elizabeth expected relief. But the knot of tension encompassing her entire body didn't ease until Caleb finally stirred and focused on her.

"There you are." She leaned over the cot from her chair and stroked his jaw. "You had me worried."

"Did I?" Caleb wondered sleepily. "Didn't mean to."

He started to move, but she held him back. "Shoulder needs some time," she warned him. "And you don't want to pull your stitches. Lana and the boys cleared the base and checked in with everyone. We're safe. Well... we're not in immediate danger, I guess." She glanced up at the lights. "Got the power back on, at least."

Caleb's pained expression eased but was replaced with worry. "Are you okay?"

"No," she admitted. "Not really. But... I'm better now. Seeing you like this..."

His jaw flexed, and his lips began to move, but she gently thumbed his lips. "I was scared. That's all."

Caleb smiled and reached for her hand. He kissed her thumb, eyes closing briefly before he sighed and moved her hand to his chest to hold it over his heart. "I told you I'd come back for you."

Elizabeth smiled. "You kept your promise. And... Lana kept hers. Jake said..."

When her words trailed off, Caleb frowned, and moved his head just enough to look around the med bay. "Where is she? Did Derek make it?"

"He's okay." Elizabeth gave a quiet snort. "He's in his quarters. Lana is... probably there, too. He's in rough shape, kind of like you. She's taking care of him."

"Ah," Caleb breathed. Maybe he saw the worry in Elizabeth's eyes, because he shrugged his good shoulder and squeezed her hand. "She could do worse. He's a good man, I think. Or, he really wants to be, and maybe that's as important."

"Maybe. I just worry about her getting attached. After Jessup."

"She's not the girl we sent off to college anymore." His eyes shifted toward the door as if he could somehow see his daughter clear across the facility. "We can't keep her sheltered. We have to let her become whoever she's growing into."

"I know." Elizabeth looked toward the door herself, trying not to be afraid of how they all had changed. "I guess that goes for us, as well."

She sat in the quiet as her husband drifted off and focused on the positives. They were alive. Her family was alive and that mattered more than anything.

CHAPTER TWENTY-EIGHT
LANA

Horse Creek Base, New United States
    Saturday, June 19th, 4:10 pm EST

Lana studied her face in the mirror. All the same features were still there, marred by fading bruises and scabbed over scrapes. Same nose as her mother's, same jaw as her father's. Same eyebrows, eyes, cheeks. Her forehead that she'd always thought was a little too big, but wore a ball cap well. Same face she'd grown up with and into.

But as she watched her reflection, she had a strange sort of distance from it. As if the mirror was a window and that the person looking at her was someone else. Someone uncertain, and suspicious—as if they didn't think she belonged there.

She closed her eyes and picked up the clippers she'd found in the supply room. She switched the appliance on, letting the vibrations travel through her fingers, into her palm, and up to her wrist. When she opened her eyes again, she stared at herself for a long moment before running the flat blade up over her temple and behind her ear.

Brown hair fell away in heavy chunks, landing on her shoulders and the floor. She took off another strip, and another, until she'd cleared the left side of her head. When she was done, she turned the clippers off, set them down on the sink's edge, and stared at herself again.

The woman in the mirror now was even less familiar but... somehow in a way that felt less threatening. As if she weren't looking at a stranger so much as a person she might get to know. A kindred spirit, maybe.

Once she'd cleaned up, she took a cool, brief shower, then dressed and returned to Derek's room. He was awake, and when he spotted her, his eyebrows rose. "Oh. Wow."

Lana smiled and sank down to the edge of his cot.

He sat up and drew his knees toward his chest to give her room. "It... looks great."

She wished that it mattered. "Thanks."

He leaned his head as if trying to get a better look at her face. "Everything okay?"

With a small effort, she made herself look at him. "I almost lost you."

Derek gave a soft huff, smiling as he reached out to touch her hand. "But you didn't."

She moved her hand just out of reach.

"This... isn't the conversation I thought it was going to be, is it?"

Lana focused on the ceiling so she didn't have to see the resignation on his face. "Derek... I like you a lot. I'm glad that you're getting better, that I *didn't* lose you. But I'm not sure I can sort through my feelings with all of this going on."

She exhaled long and slow. "I can't afford to care. I can't *not* want to lose someone. Not right now. I almost let my dad go on without me. I was so..."

Derek gave her time as she struggled to find the words. "The thought of coming back and finding you dead, finding out that you'd died alone, and I hadn't been there... I can't have that kind of thing weighing on me."

He leaned back, resting against the wall.

When he didn't reply, Lana stood from the cot. "I'm sorry."

"Don't be," he said finally, quietly.

She risked a look at him. He had a sad half-smile on his lips. "I'm not gonna wait on you. But that doesn't mean I'm letting you leave me behind. Just so you know."

Lana pursed her lips, resisting a smile, and shrugged. "It's a free country, still."

With that, she left him there to rest and headed down the hall.

Horse Creek Base, New United States
Saturday, July 3rd, 10:10 am EST

"I wish you'd stay." Washington hefted the pack over Caleb's shoulder.

He tested the weight of it on his leg. The wound really needed another week or so before he put it through its paces, but the weather was good, and Caleb didn't want to get stuck when it turned again.

In the two weeks since he'd mostly recovered, he'd been thinking about what happened next. Even let himself consider the possibility of staying at the base, finding some way to make it work. Maybe rebuild some-how. It was borderline delusional, though. There wasn't anything to rebuild, let alone create.

He smiled at Washington, who still seemed to be

most comfortable in his fatigues. "I'm not gonna say it isn't tempting," he admitted. "But we have to move on. If it was just me..."

"I know." Washington nodded. "You got your family to look after."

Caleb's shoulder still hurt, and it didn't move the way it used to, but the pain wasn't crippling anymore. It was as good a time as any to get going. If he used a stick to shift the weight, he could hike. He smiled at the man. "What are you gonna do here?"

Washington's lips pressed together a little more tightly. "Maybe set up some checkpoints between here and where people are coming in from the coast to direct them our way. Try and see what supplies we can scrounge up, maybe get a water purification system running."

He glanced down the hall. "We got an environmental engineer who thinks he might be able to get something working, and he's willing to stick with us. There are still a lot of people moving west, but... not a lot of people looking out for them."

Caleb buckled the pack's strap across his chest and slung his rifle over his good shoulder. There was nothing else for him to do except meet his family at the elevator. He limped forward and extended a hand. They shook, and he held Washington's hand tight. "Be careful of kings and shiny crowns."

Washington shook his head. "Don't think that'll be a problem, Staff Sergeant."

He let the man's hand go. "It's just Machert, now. I think I'll steer clear of all that from here on out."

They moved to the door and out to the corridor. Washington fell into step beside him. "When you get out west, if you do run across the military—the *actual* US military, that is—make sure and tell them we're out here. It would be good to have some support."

"If I get the chance, I will. But... don't you think if they *were* out there, we'd have seen them already?"

Washington shrugged. "No telling what they're dealing with. Gotta stay hopeful."

They turned a corner, and found Liz, Lana, and Derek waiting for them at the elevator door. It was open, and all three of them were geared up to go.

"Just waiting on you, old man," Lana said.

Caleb smiled as he ushered them into the elevator. He turned to face Private Washington and took a last look at the corridor—at the base itself, and all the possibility he might be walking away from. It really was tempting.

Not as tempting as finding real, long-term safety for his family, though. He waved. "Good luck here."

"Same to you, Machert." The soldier swiped his key card over the pad by the door and the elevator closed before lurching upward. In another minute, they stood outside in the pale, chill morning. Caleb looked at his daughter, the side of her scalp shaved, the rest of her hair pinned tight to her head in a series of braids that ended in a tight knot at the base of her skull.

Elizabeth took his hand. "West?"

He looked past her to Derek. "Sure you wanna do this, son? Might not be possible to come back."

"I'm sure, sir." Derek's eyes moved to Lana, and Caleb figured he probably meant it.

"Alright." Caleb tugged Elizabeth's hand. "Let's see what's out there for us."

Cheyenne Mountain Complex
  Colorado Springs, CO
  Saturday, July 3rd, 11:02 am MST

"Sir?"

President Daniels looked up from his Bible to see his Chief of Staff at the door. He slipped his bookmark into the pages and closed the book over it. "Come in, Pete. What have you got?"

Pete Camby came through the door fully and closed it behind him. He approached the desk like he was walking up to a casket at a funeral. He clutched a rolled paper in his hand, some report or another. A bad one, Daniels assumed.

They were all bad these days, to be fair.

"The... reports on the water table analysis." Pete unrolled the paper as if his hands were arthritic and didn't want to uncurl, and laid it on the President's desk.

"I take it the news is bad," Daniels guessed.

"There's some variance," Pete started, "but overall, the average pH of the rainfall that we've managed to sample across six states is around two point five."

Science had never been President Daniels favorite subject, but he knew that was low enough to be a problem. "Acid rain."

Pete nodded. "More acidic than we've recorded before, sir. According to the meteorological team, more than in recorded history."

"How long will it last?"

"It's already improving." It seemed hopeful—until Pete stuffed his hands in his pockets and stared at the floor, the way he did when he had even worse news. "But the damage is done. Between the dropped temperature, the damage to crops and to the soil across about eighty percent of the arable land..."

He trailed off.

"Just tell me."

"There are some corn crops in the Midwest that may be hardy enough to survive the next few months and it looks like a large swath of Colorado might be arable. Thanks to the subsidies, it's mostly a matter of volume, but the acidity in the water table means that fish are dying out, and livestock on the eastern half of the US—"

"We're going to run out of food," Daniels finished for him.

Pete stared at the report and nodded. "It will be over

a decade before most of the land is arable again. Supply lines were already a problem. General Ainsworth has ordered a new inventory of the supplies here and is going to roll out a new rationing schedule."

As if already anticipating the tightening belt, President Daniel's stomach growled loudly. He sighed. "Make sure you tell him to count me like anyone else. I haven't seen Lieutenant Yaeger today—was he out sick? There's a private filling in for him."

Pete's lips thinned. "He... his wife passed away. Pneumonia. It was a persistent infection, came and went. She had respiratory failure last night, around two in the morning."

An ache wormed its way deep into President Daniels's heart. He'd barely noticed the young Lieutenant's absence until halfway through the day, and then hadn't had time to inquire. "I see. Anything else, Pete?"

"Not at the moment, Sir," Pete said. "There's an intelligence briefing in about one hour."

"That late already?" the President wondered. He waved Pete off. "I know, I know. I'll be optimistic. But for now, I'd like a little time alone, please."

There'd been a time when a President of the United States could never have made such a request. Now, though, there was never a shortage of pressing matters, and not nearly the staff to attend them.

Pete eyed him as if he might have something else to say, but only dipped his head and withdrew a few steps. "Of course, sir."

Daniels waited until Pete was gone to breathe again.

He sat back in his chair and traced the embossed shape of the cross on the cover of his bible. Somehow, he'd thought that cracking it open and reading through it again after all these years would give him... peace, or wisdom, or at least some sense of surrender. A piety that would ease the burden on his spirit.

But it hadn't worked. Not yet, at any rate. Maybe it wasn't going to.

Stretched out before him, he could *see* the end of his country. The onslaught was just too much. Maybe they could have pulled through the storms and the sunless sky. They might have gathered their people together, made pockets of civilization under conditions that would be difficult, but not impossible.

But without food, and without the ability to grow more in any kind of real volume, none of that would matter. People would starve. But before they did, hunger would drive them to madness. Whatever chaos they'd seen until now, it had been just the beginning. The first rumblings of what was coming.

"God help us," he whispered, and for the first time since he was a child, he really meant it as a genuine plea. Because nothing short of divine intervention could save them from what was coming.

Subscribe to Harley's newsletter to be notified when book three in *Falling Skies* is released.

www.harleytate.com/subscribe

In the meantime, if you are new to my work and are interested in more, check out my *After the EMP* series:

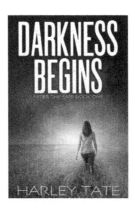

If the power grid fails, how far will you go to survive?

Madison spends her days tending plants as an agriculture student at the University of California, Davis. She plans to graduate and put those skills to work only a few hours from home in the Central Valley. The sun has always been her friend, until now.

When catastrophe strikes, how prepared will you be?

Tracy starts her morning like any other, kissing her husband Walter goodbye before heading off to work at the local public library. She never expects it to end fleeing for her life in a Suburban full of food and water. Tackling life's daily struggles is one thing, preparing to survive when it all crashes down is another.

The end of the world brings out the best and worst in all of us.

With no communication and no word from the government, the Sloanes find themselves grappling with the end of the modern world all on their own. Will Madison and her friends have what it takes to make it back to Sacramento and her family? Can Tracy fend off looters and thieves and help her friends and neighbors survive?

The EMP is only the beginning.

ALSO BY HARLEY TATE

NUCLEAR SURVIVAL

First Strike (exclusive newsletter prequel)

Southern Grit:

Brace for Impact

Escape the Fall

Survive the Panic

Northern Exposure:

Take the Hit

Duck for Cover

Ride it Out

Western Strength:

Bear the Brunt

Shelter in Place

Make the Cut

AFTER THE EMP

Darkness Falls (exclusive newsletter prequel)

Darkness Begins

Darkness Grows

Darkness Rises

Chaos Comes

Chaos Gains

Chaos Evolves

Hope Sparks

Hope Stumbles

Hope Survives

▭

NO ORDINARY DAY

No Ordinary Escape

No Ordinary Day

No Ordinary Getaway

No Ordinary Mission

▭

Find all of Harley's releases on Amazon today: www.amazon.com/author/harleytate.

ACKNOWLEDGMENTS

Thank you for reading book two of the *Falling Skies* series. I hope you are enjoying reading the story as much as I enjoyed creating it.

As I've mentioned before, a few liberties have been taken, especially with place names and other minor details in writing this novel. I hope you don't hold it against me!

If you enjoyed this book and have a moment, please consider leaving a review on Amazon. Every one helps new readers discover my work and helps me keep writing the stories you want to read.

Until next time,

Harley

When the world as we know it falls apart, how far will you go to survive?

Harley Tate writes edge-of-your-seat post-apocalyptic fiction exploring what happens when ordinary people are faced with impossible choices.

The apocalypse is only the beginning.

Contact Harley directly at:
www.harleytate.com
harley@harleytate.com

Made in the USA
Monee, IL
28 July 2022

10371913R10142